The Fish Won't Wait!

The Fish Won't Wait!

Kate Egawa

Published by Kate Egawa

© Copyright Kate Egawa 2020

THE FISH WON'T WAIT!

All rights reserved.
The right of Kate Egawa to be identified as the author of this work has been asserted in accordance with the Copyright, Designs and Patents Act 1988.

No part of this publication may be reproduced, stored in a retrieval system, or transmitted, in any form or by any means, electronic, mechanical, photocopying, recording or otherwise, nor translated into a machine language, without the written permission of the publisher.

This is a work of fiction. Names, characters, places and incidents are the product of the author's imagination or are used fictitiously. Any resemblance to actual persons, living or dead, events or locales is entirely coincidental.

Condition of sale. This book is sold subject to the condition that it shall not, by way of trade or otherwise, be lent, re-sold, hired out or otherwise circulated in any form of binding or cover other than that in which it is published and without a similar condition including this condition being imposed on the subsequent purchaser.

ISBN 979-8-691-66847-0

Contents

Lockdown. Week 1 1
Week 2 14
Week 3 29
Week 4 38
Week 5 51
Week 6 59
Week 7 82
Week 8 103
Epilogue 105

This story was written in an attempt to maintain a degree of sanity during the long days and even longer weeks of Lockdown 2020. My intention was purely to provide brief entertainment for my family and friends during this very difficult time. It is loosely and affectionately based on people and events in my life that some readers may recognise. I would like to stress that my characters and their various goings on in this story are meant to be read as fictional and bear no actual relationship to the real people who inspired them. However I would like to send a huge thank you to all, including the cats, for the inspiration!

For Mom and Dad

with love

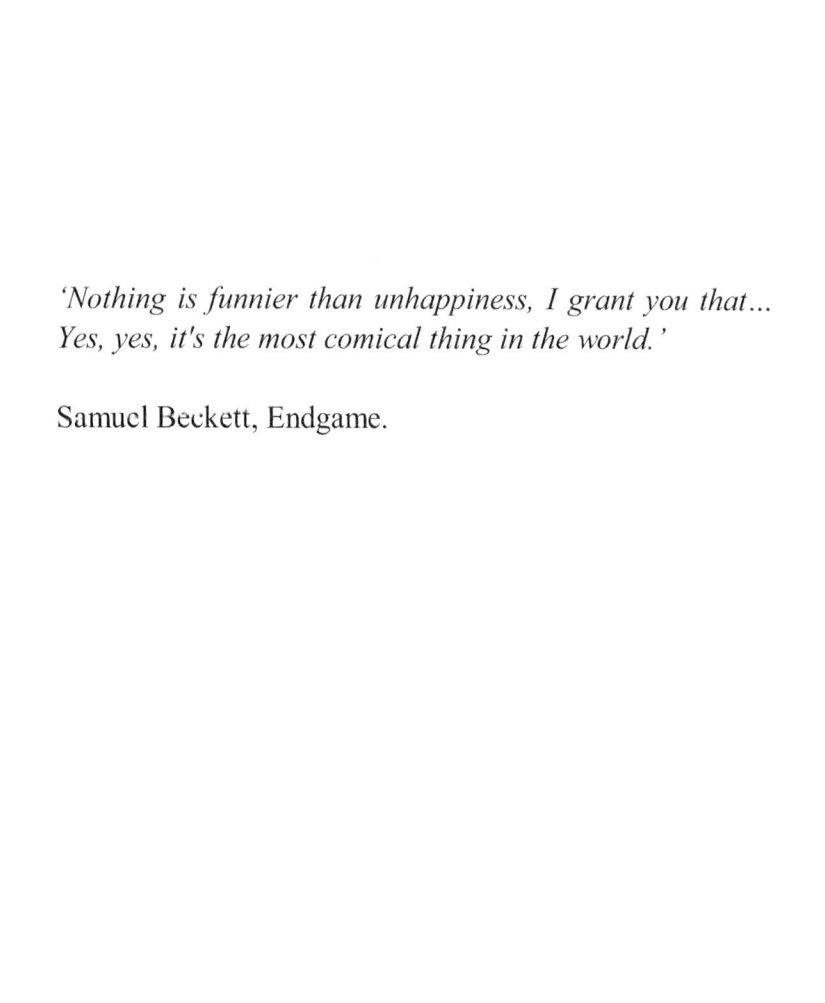

*'Nothing is funnier than unhappiness, I grant you that...
Yes, yes, it's the most comical thing in the world.'*

Samuel Beckett, Endgame.

Lockdown. Week 1.

March 23rd. 7pm.

'Ohhhhhh!' a loud wail emits from Marge's slightly red stained mouth.

'Ohhhhhhh… Tony!! Tony!! Come and listen to this! It's starting... the Lockdown is starting!'

Marge, sitting on her green leather reclining chair with a half drunk Campari in her glass, peers at the television set through her thick glasses.

'It's all over!'

The grim sounds of Boris Johnson's Eton tones ring around the room like the tolling of a death bell. His hands clasping and grasping at thin air. His shoulders hunch forward and his piercing eyes stare out at Marge, into her very soul.

> *'There won't be enough ventilators, there won't be enough intensive care beds, there won't be enough doctors and nurses…'*

'TONY!!! TONY!!'

Tony peers in around the living room door, a grimy tea-towel is flung over his shoulder and he wears a grubby apron. There are puffs of white flour all over his dark blue trousers.

'What is it now? I'm in the middle of my cake!'

'Listen,' says Marge. 'Listen to Boris... it's all over Tony! Life as we know it... all over.'

'For God's sake why do we have to listen to this? Boris bloody Johnson... what do you mean all over?'

'Listen Tony...'

Boris's voice goes on with a concerning tone,

> *'you should not be meeting friends. If your friends ask you to meet you should say no.'*

'What about work Tony? How am I going to go to work? I have to see my patients.'

> *'Use food delivery services where you can…if you don't follow the rules the police will have the powers to enforce them.'*

'Listen to that Tony…'

> *'We will immediately close all shops selling non essential goods...'*

'That's my shopping trip gone with Barbara!' wails Marge, her one empty hand raises up to her mouth which hangs open in horror.

> *'We will stop all social events including weddings, baptisms and other ceremonies... but excluding funerals...'*

'Bloody hell Marge! We can only go to funerals? Typical! They chose the most miserable option!'

'Cause there's going to be a lot of funerals Tony - a lot of funerals...'

'At present there are just no easy options. The way ahead is hard and it is true that many lives will sadly be lost.'

'Oh God this is getting worse Tony! We're all going to die!!' Marge drinks up the rest of her Campari with a large gulp.

'Can you get me another one Tony….my mother will be turning in her grave.'

'Don't overreact Marge, this will be over before you know it! Things won't change that much, you'll see. One has to keep things in perspective. It'll only be a few weeks.'

'Each and every one of us is directly enlisted...'

'God he sounds like Churchill! It's the war again Marge! Rally the troops!!'

'This is not funny Tony. How are we going to eat? We'll run out of food. We are going to starve in our own home…'

'Good job we've got plenty of wine Marge, at least we'll die happy...' Tony laughs loudly at his own joke.

'You're not taking this seriously!'

'... protect the NHS and save many many thousands of lives.'

'It'll be fine Marge- no-one will know if we pop out for a bit... I'm playing golf tomorrow...'

Marge sits up straight in her chair and gives her husband one of her withering looks. She points her finger at him.

'No Tony... you are NOT playing golf- don't you understand what he said? You're not to catch this thing! The golf course will be closed anyway.'

'No golf? Bloody hell Marge! This is a right bloody mess. This is supposed to be the 'modern world'. We're going back to the dark ages. The age of plagues and medieval witchery. Spinoza wouldn't have put up with this! I blame the Tories. If the government had seen this coming earlier none of this would have happened!'

There is an angry pause as they both stare blankly at the television.

A loud peeping sound suddenly erupts causing Marge to jump in surprise and almost drop her Campari glass. It appears to be coming from Tony's trouser pocket.

'Good God! My nerves are shot to pieces!' Marge wipes her brow with the back of her hand and signs loudly.

'That's my fish,' says Tony pulling a timer out of his pocket. 'It's done.'

Hearing the word 'fish' Chekhov the cat wanders in and surveys the scene with hopeful curiosity.

'Dinner will be in five minutes precisely!' Tony heads back into the kitchen with a renewed sense of purpose.

The phone rings.

'That'll be Jess...'says Marge.

'You're not to be on that phone for long - dinner's

nearly ready! Bloody phone always ringing...' shouts Tony from the kitchen.

He can feel his skin starting to prickle. Tony has an intense hatred of phones. His blood starts to boil at the very sound of a phone. This affliction has developed steadily over many years of overhearing Marge on what seems like endless dull phone calls from work, family, friends and whoever else.

Marge fumbles with the phone and presses the answer button. She opens the front door and wanders out into the drive in her socks. Reception is very bad in the house.

'Hello? Hello! Yes, we're fine love, yes I've seen the news… awful…awful isn't it! Yes... I don't know... we'll have to sort something out... don't worry... how are the children?... Oh yes, oh really... oh no!…What will you do? School is closed... it's dreadful... yes...'

'Dinner's ready!' bellows Tony emphatically from the kitchen. 'Are you sitting up?'

'Yes ok... yes... I have to go... dinner's ready... dad's calling me…ok... yes bye then, bye, yes speak tomorrow...'

'God why does that bloody phone always ring just as dinner is ready!' shouts Tony with the force of years of repressed frustration.

'That was Jess.' Marge comes back into the house and takes a seat in her spot at the dinner table. She settles herself ready for her fish and unfolds her napkin onto her lap.

'Right- well are you sitting up? The fish is coming...'

'I'm ready... have we got any wine?'

'Yes I've got a nice bottle.'

Tony enters the dining room carrying a large frying pan of fish, followed swiftly by the cat.

'Here we are, this is bass.' he scoops up a fish, fried in flour, and places it on Marge's plate.

'Ooh lovely that's my favourite!' says Marge.

The cat positions herself on a chair next to Marge and regards the fish with an air of hopeful anticipation. Tony uncorks a bottle of red wine and pours out two glasses, handing one to Marge.

'Well here's to the Lockdown Marge. Whatever it may bring...'

'Yes, to the Lockdown... cheers! Ooh this fish looks lovely, Tony, you are clever...'

'I look after you well, don't I my love?'

'Very well Tone, I don't know what I'd do without you!'

* * *

Marge and Tony are standing on the upstairs landing peering up at the ancient grandfather clock. It once belonged to Tony's great grandfather. Delicate scenes of various castles are painted on each corner of the clock face. It is a mysterious and wonderful thing. Tony is winding it carefully using a large rusty key that hangs on a string by the shiny bronze pendulum. It emits a loud ticking noise and chimes occasionally, but its hands are completely stuck at 1 o' clock.

'Tick, tick, tick, tick...'says the clock.

'What is it trying to tell us?' asks Marge.
'It's obvious isn't it?' replies Tony...'it's broken!'

'Tick, tick, tick, tick…'

* * *

Marge is a psychiatrist. She attempted to retire on several occasions, but was unable to settle comfortably into a life of domesticity and daytime TV. Work keeps her busy, allows her to attend her beloved conferences and make her precious notes. Marge has a marvellous ability to take notes. Notes about her patients, her meetings, her conferences, interesting things she hears on the radio. Just about anything in fact.

Unfortunately, having no particular place to keep her notes, she tends to leave them scattered around the house. Over the years, piles upon piles of notes have gradually gathered on the stairs, on the landing, on the floors, on the shelves. Anywhere in fact where there is an empty space, and these days there are fewer and fewer.

This habit is certainly not encouraged by Tony. Quite the opposite in fact. Tony has developed a pathological dislike of Marge's notes. The topic of Marge's notes and their gradual spread into all corners of the house has been the focus of many heated arguments which end nowhere. Tony sees piles of notes quite regularly in his nightmares. He slips on them as he walks about the house. He treads on them as he heads to bed at night. He trips over them as he goes down the stairs. Sometimes he 'accidently' throws them away.

A large tower of BMJs (British Medical Journal) has been growing for many years by the front door. It is now about shoulder height. Tony frequently attempts to throw them away but is thwarted by Marge and her desperate pleas that she needs them. All of them. Each and every one.

Marge is sitting at the dining room table peering at a laptop surrounded by a scattered array of notes and papers. The cat is sitting next to her on a fluffy cushion.

'Tony! Tony! Can you come here a minute, I need some help!'

Tony is a retired head teacher and writer. He is slouched over his laptop, sunk into the large brown leather sofa in the darkened lounge. His fingers tap loudly and urgently over the keyboard like the feet of a distressed chicken dancing on a hotplate. Tony is absorbed in his latest novel. Bach's concerto in D minor for double violins is playing at a deafening volume. Amidst this scene, Marge's voice is utterly lost.

'TONY!! TONY!! CAN YOU COME, I NEED SOME HELP,' shouts Marge again, raising her chin slightly into the air to project her voice.

Tony continues slouching, the fingers continue tapping and Bach continues playing.

Marge gets up out of her seat and wanders into the lounge calling loudly. It is very dark in the lounge and it is almost impossible to see the shadow of Tony's slouching figure in the gloom. Through Marge's thick glasses it is totally impossible, so she wanders off into the garden to check in the writing hut on the Back Land.

The Back Land is a wild place which Tony and Marge have cultivated at the rear of their garden to share their delight of wild flowers. Unfortunately due to years of neglect, brambles and thorns have rather overtaken the flowers and are spreading as fast as Marge's notes.

Seated in the middle of the Back Land is Tony's writing hut. It is a small wooden structure, hexagonal in shape. A few years ago it looked splendid, situated amongst bluebells, primulas and snowdrops, as idyllic as the Seven Dwarfs' cottage. But now it is embedded in a nest of rambling creepers, ivy, brambles and thorns.

One day soon perhaps, after a particularly long writing effort, Tony will end up trapped in his hut by the choking creepers and will require rescuing like the poor Sleeping Beauty from her stricken castle.

Stumbling in her slippers across this treacherous wasteland, Marge curses as she spikes her ankles. She peers in through the window of the hut and calls loudly. There is no answer. She taps a few times on the wooden door with a large twig that she has picked up on the way. Marge has a useful habit of collecting sticks for the fire. She is unable to pass a good stick without picking it up and putting it in her bag.

'TONY!! TONY!! Where are you? Oh goodness - my meeting starts in a minute!'

Marge is now feeling rather upset and she shuffles back through the brambles, through the gate and back into the garden and into the house. As she enters the lounge to put her stick in the bucket by the fire, she switches on the light and suddenly spots Tony slouching on the sofa.

'I've been all up the garden looking for you!'

'Well I'm here!'

'My ankles have got all scratched!'

'Oh dear!'

'Can you come and help me? My meeting starts in five minutes and I can't get on the thing.'

'You can't get on the thing?'

"No, can you come and have a look? Hurry!'

Tony senses that he has very little choice in the matter, so he folds his laptop closed with a large sigh and hoists himself out of the sofa.

They peer at Marge's laptop as Tony taps hopefully on a few random buttons. Marge is trying to use a new online meeting platform known as 'Zoom'. It enables people to meet face to face from the comfort of their own homes. It has the added advantage that you need only get dressed in the morning on the top half, as the bottom area remains discreetly hidden. In Marge's case it means she can wear her underskirt and odd coloured bed socks all day and not have to worry.

'There, that looks like it's done,' says Tony with an air of triumph as a square grid of smiling faces appears on the screen.

'Oh thank you!' replies Marge as she sits down ready to take notes.

As Tony heads back into the lounge there is a loud knock on the door.

'Oh God! What's this bothering me now? I'm constantly being bothered! How can I get anything done?'

Tony opens the door. A man in a very large industrial gas mask is standing approximately two meters back from the front step. There is a tool box by his leg. The thick breathing tube protruding from the front of the mask gives him the disturbing appearance of an enormous fly.

'Hello?' says Tony. 'Who are you?'

There is a vague muffling sound as the man gestures and waves in his plastic gloved hands.

'Hgbghhdfffsbmnnggggfhhh,' says the man.

'What? I can't hear you, speak up!'

There is more muffled noise and more gesturing.

'Take that bloody thing off, you look like you've been on the Front Line!'

The man pulls off his mask and reveals a worried face.

'Hello Doctor Pinkton, I've come to fix the fire. I have to be quick because I'm worried the police are gonna catch me.'

'Oh the fire - yes that's good, the smoke puffs out all over the room. What do you mean the police?'

'Well I'm not supposed to be working you see. The Lockdown rules say I can' t be working. It's not essential work you see.'

'Well it is in my opinion and I'll tell that to any police that turn up here!'

'Oh good Doctor Pinkton, can I come in?... I'm worried they will follow me here. I think they can see my van.'

'Oh yes, come in, but you'd better put your mask back on or Marge won't like it. I don't want to be getting into trouble.'

The fire-man squeezes his enormous mask back over his head and enters the house. Tony shows him the fire place in the living room and he sets to work. Tony picks up his laptop and heads upstairs to his attic hideaway where he goes when he doesn't want to be bothered.

It is dark in the lounge and the fire-man finds it hard to see, especially through the plastic visage of his mask, which is steaming up rapidly. Smoke is billowing out into the room from the fireplace. The fire-man decides to try and find a light switch. He reaches out his arms and waves them around as he edges carefully forwards searching for a wall.

After roughly five minutes of edging and waving fruitlessly around in the darkness, the fire-man starts to panic. He doesn't do well in enclosed spaces at the best of times. Oxygen levels in his mask are reducing rapidly. His breathing becomes rasping and laboured. His head starts to spin and his eyes blur over. His body sways and bends like an ear of corn in an autumn field. With a dramatic final sweep worthy of any good operatic finale, he slumps down heavily, very luckily just catching a good spot on the sofa.

'Blast it!' Marge has accidentally exited the meeting just at a critical moment when she leaned over to reach her tea.

"Blast it!!' In her panic she starts pressing random buttons and the screen goes blank.

'TONY!! HELP ME! IT'S NOT WORKING!!' she shouts as she comes out of the dining room, into the hallway and heads towards the lounge.

'TONY! HELP ME!' she shouts into the darkness.

There is a strange heavy breathing sound that stops Marge in her tracks. She freezes, eyes reaching blindly though the darkness and smoke. The heavy rasping continues, deep and regular like Darth Vader in a pivotal scene.

'Oh my God Tony! Are you alright? What's happened? Are you sick?'

Visions of Tony on a hospital ventilator flash through her mind.

In her panic Marge reaches out and switches the light on, suddenly revealing the prostrate form of the fire-man lying on the sofa gasping in his large respirator.

'AHHHHHHHHHHHH!!!!!!' she shrieks. 'AAAAAA

LOCKDOWN.WEEK 1

AAAAAHHHHHHHHHHHHHHHHHHHHHHHHHHH!!!!!!!!!'

Tony can hear a muffled scream from high up in his writing attic.

'Oh for God's sake what now?' he sighs. He gets up rather too quickly, banging his head on the low sloping ceiling. He has done this hundreds of times before, leaving a pattern of greasy blotches on the creamy white paintwork.

'Bugger it!!'

Clutching his head, Tony makes his way down the narrow winding staircase and in his haste slips on a pile of papers balancing gently on the last step.

Tony is lying on his back on the first floor landing listening as the unearthly sounds of high pitched shrieking and deep rasping float up from the room below. He looks up at the pretty paper light shade hanging overhead and his eyes are drawn curiously to a delicate netting of spiderwebs in the corner of the ceiling. He contemplates this for a moment. Then his mind turns to Spinoza.

'Humans think they are free, but they dream with their eyes open,' he mutters quietly.

Then he rolls himself over and crawls slowly on his hands and knees back upstairs to his attic, closing the door behind him.

Week 2

Jeff and Joe are sitting in their kitchen with two glasses of ice cold gin and tonic. Edna the cat is sitting comfortably on Joe's lap. She has a little orange quilted jacket on with a pink fur wrap and a white diamonte collar. She is a rare Sphynx breed which means she is entirely bald and has many folds of loose wrinkly skin. She has huge ears like a bat, deep olive green eyes and a gravely disapproving expression. Edna has a tendency to feel the cold so she has her own special wardrobe with an array of tiny hats, coats, jumpers and leg warmers. Jeff and Joe are utterly devoted to her, despite the fact that most people find her appearance highly challenging.

'How many bookings do we have for this week?' asks Jeff anxiously.

'Let me check…hold on a mo...'replies Joe peering over his laptop.

'We've got Bertie on Thursday, morning and evening, Jelly and Jasper on Tuesday morning, then Kewpie and Bonnie … we've also got Stalin on Wednesday around 6pm…it looks like Chekhov is still on for Saturdays…then a late one with Mr Spock on Sunday at 10pm. We've had a lot of cancellations - people are just not going out!'

WEEK 2

'Ooh a late one with Mr Spock! Fabulous! He's such a darling I can't wait!' replies Jeff. Mr Spock is a large long haired ginger tom who adores Jeff and Joe's visits. That's not surprising as he is spoiled rotten with fishy treats and endless games of chasing string.

'We're down so many bookings with the Lockdown, I don't know how we're going to hold out. God- things are so unfair! We've worked so hard to make 'Rainbow Paws' a success and now I don't know what will happen. After all, who needs cat sitters when we're all stuck at home?' Joe draws Edna in for a rather tight cuddle which causes her to squeak.

'Don't worry my love, everything will work out just fine, you'll see! Remember you've always got me and Edna. We'll look after you,' reassures Jeff calmly, sipping his gin.

'I know... I know... we just need to boost our income... think of new ways forward. We don't know how long this thing will go on.'

'Ok - let's think outside the box - what do people need in the Lockdown? How about videos of their cats to get them though the long lonely days? We could make online memories? Mugs, photocards…how about personalised get well soon cards with cats on? I know… 'don't CATch the virus' cards!! Get it? CATch the virus!!' Jeff laughs loudly which makes Edna jump and dig her claws into Joe's leg.

'OWWW!! Edna!!! Ok, let's make a note of that...'Joe taps on the keyboard. 'Or what about zoom chats with owners and their pets? We could host pet parties! We could do cat Bingo for the old folks!'

'Yeah!! Good one,' says Jeff. 'How about cat quiz

evenings? I've heard people are doing quizzes and stuff...'

'Yeah I like it!' Joe taps that idea in. 'We can make it all about cat trivia!!'

'Oh my God! I've got it!! Listen to this... you're gonna love this one...matching owner and cat face masks!!'

'YES!! You are brilliant Jeff! I love it!! We can make one for Edna for the photo shoot. Edna you are going to look gorgeous!!'

As their glasses chink together, Jeff and Joe raise a hopeful toast for the continued success of 'Rainbow Paws' in Lockdown. Edna receives a fishy treat which she gobbles down noisily.

'ONWARDS AND UPWARDS!!'

* * *

'Hello Jess, yes Dad and I are fine. Shall we go for our walk soon? Yes okay come over and we'll set off.'

> *There is a soft and cheerful chiming from the grandfather clock upstairs. It seems to be heralding spring.*
> *'Bong... bong... bong...'*

Marge and her daughter Jess go for a walk around the local park every morning. Jess has now taken hundreds upon hundreds of photos of ducks, swans, geese and other feathered water fowl that occupy the lake. Two coot mothers are sitting patiently on their large twiggy nests. Spring is in the air and the cherry blossoms are blooming with full force. Bluebells scatter a carpet of blue and white among the Victorian graves.

Later on in the day Marge repeats the same walk with Tony, breaking the one walk a day rule, but as she says, no-one's going to know.

Jess lives with her two teenage daughters about two minutes drive away from her parents. She has taken on the shopping duties for them which keeps her busy, as well as teaching adults in a local Birmingham college. She has had to adapt to online lessons which is extremely challenging especially as most of her learners don't have access to technology.

Her younger daughter Ada spends her days on the laptop in her bedroom at 'virtual' school. It works fairly well and there are certain very useful bonuses. Pupils do have the added advantage of being able to 'switch off' the teacher if the lesson becomes tedious. If you get picked on to answer a difficult question, the 'mute' button can suddenly 'break'. It breaks fairly often for Ada. They can also bunk off PE without the teacher knowing. On one occasion Ada was asked to film herself doing the long jump in her room and send it in. Fortunately the teacher quickly realised this was a hopeless task and gave up on the idea. So virtual school really does have its advantages. Jess is also pleased because she avoids the hour and a half school run everyday.

Jess's elder daughter Rowan has had to come back from university in London where she is studying Fine Art. She is very upset indeed by the whole Lockdown thing. She spends her day times sleeping and night times on Netflix thinking about how life would be so much better drinking in the pub with her friends.

THE FISH WON'T WAIT!

* * *

Jess and Marge are sitting on the green chairs in the garden underneath a large Copper Beech. It is a magnificent tree which overlooks the main lawn. It must be at least one hundred and fifty years old. Tiny leaf buds hang on the branches, poised to open and reveal their golden brilliance. Jess is trying to teach Marge how to set up a Zoom meeting. It is very difficult as Jess has to stay a safe two metres away. Marge is taking copious notes. This is proving very tricky indeed.

* * *

Tony had spent a long three hours in the kitchen perfecting his Persian lamb rissoles, a recipe which he had discovered in last week's Financial Times. Everything is in control. He has three timers set up in his pockets for the fish, rissoles and beetroot fritters. He'd luckily managed to substitute the pine nuts for cashews which he'd eventually found in the deepest recesses of the pantry. A few years out of date, but it doesn't matter. The table is laid and the wine is open.

Cooking is a fine art for Tony. As Michelangelo mastered his carving chisel, Tony mastered his spatula. His culinary life began when he and Marge were first married. He quickly realised she did not show an aptitude for cooking. That infamous evening when the vicar came over for dinner and the roast chicken skidded across the floor, is now seared painfully in Tony's memory. It became clear that if life was to hold any kind of culinary pleasure he would have to take over at the helm. Steer the ship into more exotic waters. As far away from macaroni cheese and Hungarian goulash as physically possible.

Tony sits in his kitchen chair, a glass of whisky (a 25 year old vintage Glenmorange, no less) with an air of complete and utter satisfaction.

Marge is adding the finishing touches to the table by putting out the napkins they used yesterday, and cleaning a small dried spill of wine by rubbing it with her finger.

The phone rings.

'Oh God no...' mutters Tony, his heart sinking, looking up from his paper. It is just three and half minutes to the fish and this was just not the time.

'Hello?' says Marge pushing the answer button firmly. 'Hello? Yes ... I'll just take you outside... I can't hear anything…'

Marge opens the front door and wanders out into the drive in her odd coloured bed socks.

'Oh yes, that's better.' One of her patients is having some kind of crisis.

'Oh dear, yes… yes… has she been eating? No?... Have you done the bloods... ?'

Tony gets up out of his chair and opens the oven door to inspect the lamb rissoles. They are bubbling nicely. It's time for the fish. He switches the gas on and heats olive oil in a large frying pan. The bass fillets are already floured on a plate. He carefully lowers the fish into the pan and resets his timer for two minutes twenty seconds exactly. One has to be precisely exact with cooking. Time is the key.

'Yes, well I see that is very difficult isn't it. Have you talked to the mother? I think we should do a section...'

Marge has spotted a nice robin as she discusses her

patient and is now heading out of the driveway and onto the pavement.

'Can you get the paperwork to me… yes I can do it … email it to me now and I'll have a look…'

Marge can just see a potentially excellent stick over there on the side of the road, which she cannot help but investigate further. She heads off down the road.

Back in the kitchen the timer is peeping loudly in Tony's pocket. The fish is done.

'Dinner's ready!!!' shouts Tony. There is no response.

'DINNER'S READY!!!!!' he shouts again.

He puts down the frying pan and opens the sliding garden door.

'DINNER'S READY!!!' he shouts into the garden. Tony can feel the blood rising into his head rapidly and his cheeks turning the shade of the beetroot rissoles.

Marge reaches the stick and picks it up. Just ahead is another very nice specimen.

'Yes ... that sounds like a good plan... we'll go ahead with that. I'll speak to the mother and explain…'

The fish is now a whole eight minutes thirty seconds overdue. Tony has been calling all over the house and garden. He has a big wet patch on his trousers where he spilt his whisky and two timers are now going off in his pocket at the same time. Tony has reached his mental and emotional limits. He explodes with apocalyptic force at the bottom of the stairs.

'WHERE THE BLOODY HELL ARE YOU? THE DINNER IS READY THE FISH HAS NOW BEEN WAITING FOR EIGHT MINUTES FORTY NINE SECONDS THIS IS TOTALLY OUTRAGEOUS THEY WOULDN'T HAVE TO PUT UP WITH THIS AT THE

WEEK 2

SAVOY DO YOU THINK GORDON RAMSAY HAS TO PUT UP WITH THIS WHAT IF HIS GUESTS JUST DISAPPEARED WHEN THE FISH IS READY DO YOU THINK HE'D JUST SAY OH DEAR NEVER MIND THAT'S FINE I'LL JUST COOK IT ALL AGAIN TOMORROW WHEN THE GUESTS CAN BE BOTHERED TO TURN UP NO HE WOULDN'T WOULD HE DON'T EVER EXPECT ME TO COOK THE DINNER AGAIN THAT IS IT I QUIT IT'S ALL OVER I RESIGN THE CHEF HAS GONE IT'S BAKED BEANS FOR YOU TOMORROW AND EVERY OTHER DAY FROM NOW ON…'

Marge tucks two sticks under her arm and sets off a bit further down the road thinking that one or two more would be very useful.

Tony has now reached the resignation stage of his breakdown and decides to eat the dinner alone. He picks up the pan and heads towards the dining room. As he walks in he notices the cat sitting in Marge's chair at the table, looking expectantly.

'Oh good! Are you ready for your fish?' smiles Tony as he carefully places a fish on the plate in front of the cat.

'Would you like some mayonnaise?'

* * *

Cap is packing the lawn mower into his trailer. During the Second World War he served as a Corporal in the RAF, stationed in India and Burma. His heroic rescue of his comrades in the heavy bombing campaign in Burma led to his nickname Cap. He has now been a gardener for more than forty years and is keeping going despite his many physical challenges. He suffers from a bent spine which has become increasingly worse over the past three or so years, leaving him with a severe bent back and prominent shoulder hunch. His left leg has also been playing up now for the past few months and causing him to limp quite dramatically. Since his wife died eight years ago he has devoted himself to his gardening. Despite these setbacks, Cap is a cheery soul and built as strong as an ox. Nothing will get in the way of him and his mowing.

Cap loves mowing more than any of his other gardening tasks. He is never happier than when he is cutting perfectly straight lines across a green lawn. There is a fine art to mowing that Cap has perfected over the years. The blades must be sharpened and waxed, the depth of the cut must be at the exact proportion to the length of the grass. The line must be at the exact angle, the speed must be just so. Cap likes to think of himself as the samurai of mowing. As the samurai has his sword, so Cap has his mower. He is a craftsman of the highest order. He has mowing in his soul.

On this occasion he is off to mow the lawn of his loyal customers the good doctors Pinkton who employ him on a regular basis.

Cap pulls up with his trailer and unloads the mower with the greatest of care. He lets himself through to the garden via the side gate. He wheels the mower to the lawn and sets it aside while he inspects the lawn meticulously. Cap surveys the scene with his expert eye. He crouches low to get the full 'snails eye' perspective of the length of the grass. He runs his hand tenderly over the surface of the lawn to feel its moisture content. His eyes close as the sweet musky scent of grass enters his nostrils. In a trance like state he flattens himself out face down as he starts to feel the connection with Great Mother Earth. It is a ritual of deep seriousness and gravity. This all takes time and the Master is not inclined to rush. Especially as he is being paid by the hour.

Marge and Tony are watching from the kitchen window.

'Who is that?' asks Marge.

'I've no idea,' replies Tony.

'What is he doing?'

'How should I know?'

'Can you go and find out?'

'No.'

'Tony! I don't like the look of him.'

'Why don't you go?'

'Me? He might be dangerous!'

'So it's okay for me to put myself in danger... ?'

'I've only got my socks on...'

'Okay fine... I'll go but get the phone ready you may need to call for help.'

'Can you give me a signal?'

'Yes- if I do this (waves) that means you should call the police at once.'

'Okay don't worry Tony, I'll be watching.'

Tony opens the sliding door to the garden and steps outside. Cap is lying face down on the lawn sweeping his arms to and fro in a slow regular motion.

'Ahem,' Tony clears his throat.

'Ahem,' Tony clears his throat again slightly louder.

'AHEM,' Tony shouts with force, this time making

Cap startle out of his reverie and sit up on the grass, blinking in the sunshine.

'What do you think you are doing?' Cap demands, frowning crossly. He has been awoken from his spiritual oneness with the Greater Force at a very critical moment.

'Er... well I was just popping out to see... er ... if you needed anything.' Tony was feeling slightly threatened and didn't want to make the situation worse.

'No, everything is just fine thank you,' replies Cap eager to get back to his job.

'Er... okay... if you're sure. Then I'll just ... er ... leave you to get on then.'

'Yes, leave me to get on, that would be very good.' Cap lies down again.

'Er actually I was wondering... who are you, in fact...?'

'I've been mowing your lawn for the past twenty years! Cap... Cap the gardener.'

'Oh Cap! Last time we met must have been about twenty years ago! We're always away when you come over. You've changed a bit since then.' Tony vaguely remembers Cap as a well built lithe fellow, not the rather bent, hunched figure in front of him.

'Yes, well, twenty years is a long time. Do you mind?...I do have a job to do...'

'Righty ho! So sorry! Off I go then...'Tony spots Marge at the window and smiles and waves to indicate that everything is fine.

That's the wave that Marge has been waiting for. She starts to panic and dials 999.

'Hello, yes... police... yes there's a dangerous man in

my garden... yes come at once! Hurry!'

She replaces the receiver.

Tony steps through the sliding door.

'Well, that went well,' he says. 'Everything seems just fine.'

* * *

Marge is watering a small cactus on the window sill and Tony is at the small baby grand piano playing a Dave Brubeck improvisation. There is a knock at the front door. Nothing happens. There is another louder knock. Marge puts down the watering can and answers the door. It is Riya from next door, wearing a face mask.

'Oh, hello Riya! How lovely to see you!'

'Hello Marge! I hope you are keeping well. I've just popped round to see if you'd like me to drop off some lunch for you and Tony after I get back from the Gurdwara every day. You see I go there every morning to make food for the staff at the Queen Margaret hospital. We have plenty of it.'

'Oh my goodness, well that would be very kind...'

'Well that's settled then, I'll leave it on the door step starting from tomorrow. I'll knock so you'll know it's there.'

'Well thank you so much Riya, that is so very kind of you...'

'No problem at all... see you then...'

* * *

PC Jones at Thornhurst police station has just received a

call from a rather hysterical woman called Marge about a dangerous man in the garden. He picks up his radio.

'1-2-3 control, Thornhurst Road, copy over...'

PC Patel is sipping a coffee from his flask in his patrol car hidden under a large bush at the edge of Muggins Park. He is observing the goings on with the utmost scrutiny. If any unsuspecting pedestrian breaks the 2 metre distancing rules, Patel is poised to move in and restore order at a moments notice. PC Patel takes his role as constable with deadly seriousness and deep pride. This is his third year in service and he is looking for promotion. He deserves promotion. He is dedicated, he is poised for action, he has the eyes of an eagle and the cunning of a fox. His aunty Aisha works as a frontline Covid nurse and PC Patel is making it his personal mission to protect the NHS. His radio beeps and his hand startles, spilling his coffee on his trousers.

'Shit!' he picks up the radio receiver, mopping a tissue over his crotch.

'Patel 1-2-3 copying over...' he replies.

'Suspicious intruder at 42 Chestnut Drive.'

'Roger... I'm on the job. Over and out.'

PC Patel gulps down the last bit of coffee and screws the top on his flask in a flash. He flips on the sirens, revs up loudly and swerves out of the park into the road with an unnerving screech that sends an innocent group of pigeons leaping frantically into the air. All that remains is a small cloud of exhaust smoke lingering by the bush.

Marge is back at her computer and Tony is loading the dishwasher. Cap is moving the mower steadily up and down the lawn with trancelike precision. A siren can be heard in the distance gradually increasing in volume until it is loud enough even to cause Tony to stop and pause for a moment. Then it stops.

There is a loud knock at the door and some muffled shouting.

Tony blinks with slight alarm. A siren and a knock could only mean one thing in his opinion. Trouble.

Tony tiptoes into the dining room.

'Marge, Marge! I think the police are at the door... what shall we do?' he whispers.

Marge's memory suddenly flashes back to ten minutes ago and it all fits into place.

'Well, I think I phoned them Tony!'

'You did what?'

'Well you waved at me so I phoned them... I said there was an intruder.'

'You what!!! Oh dear God...'

There is the sound of heavy pounding on the front door and some shouting that sounds like, 'OPEN UP NOW... POLICE...OPEN UP......'

'They'll break the bloody door down Marge!! Do something!!' Tony is agitated and his face is going red.

'Well let them in then!' says Marge calmly. 'We've got some cake...'

Tony and Marge hurry out into the hall. Tony unclips the latch and the door flies open allowing PC Patel to hurl unexpectedly and violently into the hallway. He lands face first onto the long Turkish rug, knocking into the tall pile of BMJs stacked in the corner like a Leaning Tower of Pisa. Marge and Tony watch in horror as the tower bends and sways then slowly and inevitably topples over, burying PC Patel alive in a crushing mound of medical enlightenment.

'Good lord!' comments Marge.

'Hello Officer,' says Tony cautiously.

PC Patel remains motionless for a few long moments while he tries to take stock of the situation. This has not been the scenario he was hoping for and now he is lying prostrate on the floor with a potentially broken nose. Gradually he gathers himself together and is helped slowly into the lounge by Marge on one arm and Tony on the other.

'Oh dear!' remarks Marge peering at his rapidly swelling nose. 'I'll get some peas out of the freezer.'

Tony is left alone with the officer to explain the error of situation, that his wife had not recognised the gardener and thought he was a very suspicious character... her eyesight is dreadful... she's got very thick glasses... he had tried to stop her but you know how it is sometimes... when Marge makes up her mind there's nothing to be done.

PC Patel has heard enough and by the time Marge reappears with half a packet of frozen peas he is getting into his patrol car and heading back to the station for a much needed cigarette and a lie down in one of the empty cells. Unwittingly entering 42 Chestnut Drive, he has broken the 2 metre rule and for that he is deeply upset. That is a house to keep a very close eye on. A very close eye indeed.

'He seems like a nice young man,' says Marge sipping her large Campari.

Week 3

Tony and Marge are sitting in the kitchen with their morning coffee. Tony is checking an Otto Lenghi recipe book for ideas for dinner.

Marge is reading the Daily Mail that she found on a bench at the park.

'Boris is a Fighter, he'll pull through,' reads the headline.

'Oh no! Tony have you heard that Boris is in hospital. He must have got worse!'

'Oh God! With him out of action who do we have left steering this ship through the stinking mire? Dominic bloody Raab! Marvellous!'

'Well I hope he'll be okay, Tony. Even if it is Boris. We must hope for the best.'

'Tick... tick... tick...'goes the grandfather clock. Only time will tell.

* * *

Jess has been queuing to get into Asda for the past hour. It is 8am in the morning. The queue stretches out around the car park. Everyone is wearing masks and plastic gloves and standing two metres apart.

There is an unusual atmosphere of calm resignation. As the security guard gives the go-ahead, Jess enters the supermarket and feels a certain sense of elation which reminds her suddenly of the moment she reached Splash Canyon at Alton Towers after queuing up for two and a half hours.

She reaches into her pocket for the shopping list. Out comes a screwed up pile of very small scraps of paper on which various items are listed in scrawly spidery handwriting. Jess sighs deeply and realises that her new role shopping for her parents is not going to be as easy as she first thought. There are now arrows all over the supermarket floor which are meant to channel the shoppers in orderly directions.

To make matters worse there are all kinds of things on this list that Jess has never heard of and even less idea where to find them... Moroccan annatto powder... fresh cordyceps mushrooms....Thai basil... daikon root... dried goji berries... bread flour.

There is no bread flour of any kind. In fact there are great holes on the supermarket shelves where pasta, hand soap, toilet rolls and other basics should be. Tony will be lucky if he gets a pint of milk let alone a gogi berry.

The lack of flour is extremely worrying. Tony bakes a new cake every other day. He also bakes his own bread. The thought of having to explain to her dad that there just isn't any flour fills Jess with dread.

Sometimes it is possible to find solace in the most unlikely of places. For Jess it is found at the Esso petrol station at the bottom of the main road, round the corner from her house. When times get hard, Jess heads down to get petrol. After her particularly stressful trip to Asda Jess is in need of petrol to fill her ebbing spirits.

As Jess arrives at the petrol station she gets out of the car and pulls out the petrol nozzle. Over the tannoy she hears a familiar voice,

'Well there she is! I've been waiting for you... good morning my chicken!'

She looks up and sees Marv on the microphone, waving and grinning from his spot in the pay kiosk. Other customers are looking around wondering where the voice is coming from.

Marv is a wonderful mix of Afro Caribbean and Irish Gypsy Traveller. He is wearing a red Esso sweater stretched over his big rotund belly. With tight curly black hair and a beard, he looks like a cross between Father Christmas and a buddha from down the hood. His arms are hung with an array of crystal bracelets and around his neck hangs a bundle of assorted necklaces. His huge smile shows several large black holes where teeth are missing- but it doesn't matter. Jess thinks he is just sublime.

'No smiling allowed in this place,' says Marv.

'Why not?' smiles Jess getting out her purse.

'It's been banned - the boss said so. You'd better go before he sees you.'

'Aren't you the boss Marv?'

'No one is the boss. We are all born equal. Mastering others is strength. Mastering yourself is true power.' Marv is getting philosophical.

'Is that right? Have you mastered yourself Marv?' Jess taps the pay machine with her bank card.

Marv points to the sky, 'there is the mystery of life...

that's where we need to channel our energies. Just feel it - you gotta feel it, it's talking to you. You just gotta listen.'

'Just gotta listen...' repeats Jess.

'Listen to what the cosmos is telling you...'

There was a queue forming at the till and Jess felt her time was up.

'Well, Marv. I guess I'd better go, see you soon.' She heads to the door.

As she walks to the car a voice rings out over the tannoy.

'Remember - when you can't find the sunshine, be the sunshine...'

Jess and the car leave the temple of the Esso station, both feeling refuelled and satisfied for now.

Marge is sitting at her computer at the dining room table trying to set up a Zoom meeting for work. She is following her notes carefully and slowly pressing buttons on the keyboard. After about half an hour she has managed to successfully set up a meeting. Marge is feeling very proud of herself. However when she starts the meeting and nobody comes, she realises she must have forgotten something rather important... to send out the invites.

* * *

It is 1 pm and PC Patel drives slowly down Chestnut Drive. He pulls up outside number 42 for a moment and peers at the red brick house through his binoculars. He spots something sitting on the doorstep. That looks very suspicious. He gets out of the patrol car and creeps carefully up to have a closer look. There is a pot of something, some bhajis and a plate of samosas. They look very nice.

WEEK 3

PC Patel is feeling rather hungry. He picks up a samosa and sniffs it. Mmmm smells good. Mmmm tastes good.

Back in the patrol car PC Patel is feeling very satisfied. No suspicious activity today but he might have to pop by again tomorrow just in case. Probably around lunchtime.

* * *

Jess stands on the doorstep of her parent's house having delivered the daily shopping. On the edge of the step she is curious to notice a large pot of dhal, a pile of samosas and 2 onion bhajis. It smells very good. She helps herself to a bhaji.

'I'm sorry Dad but I just can't get flour... I've been everywhere I can think of. It's just nowhere to be found...'

'Oh God! That is a total disaster!' Tony says dramatically. 'How am I supposed to make my cakes and my bread?'

'Well haven't you got any left at all?'

'There's a bit but it won't go far.'

'I've got a bag at home you can have. I could check on Amazon...'

'Okay well, see what you can do. I'll have to find a new recipe... use something else...'

'Yes that sounds like an idea. Have a look in the Financial Times, I'm sure they'll be something helpful in there!'

'Are you and the girls coming for dinner? I need to cook for people who eat properly. Your mother eats like a pigeon.'

'Dad, it's Lockdown remember - we're not supposed

to be mixing together.'

'Rubbish! We can be careful. Go round the back and we'll eat in the garden. At a distance that Boris would approve of.'

'Well...'

'That's settled... see you at seven.'

* * *

Jeff and Joe are both on their hands and knees on the floor of their photography studio in the attic of their house. They are attempting to create a photo shoot to advertise their new matching cat and owner masks. A couple of silver and black umbrellas are positioned by the white back screen. An expensive Nikon camera is poised ready on a tripod.

They have cut and sewn a range of fabulous contemporary designs which the fashion loving cat owner would just die for. The only problem facing them now is Edna. Edna doesn't like the masks. In fact she hates them.

'Come on my darling, be good for Daddy...' pleads Joe, holding out another fishy treat.

Edna is sitting in a corner looking defiant. Whenever the mask approaches her head she sweeps it away with the air of a Hollywood diva. This has now been going on for over two hours. Edna is no longer able to physically ingest any more fishy treats without exploding.

'It's no good! It's just not going to work.' Jeff is utterly exhausted.

Joe closes his eyes and collapses face down on the floor,

'I can't go on... ! I can't do this any more!'

WEEK 3

'All that bloody effort and she won't bloody wear it!' Jeff lies flat on his back and puts his hands on his head in despair. 'Ahhhhhhhhhhrrrrrgggggggg!!!!!' he moans.

'I bloody hate cats,' mumbles Joe, his face buried deep into the shag pile rug.

Edna heaves up her bloated belly, glances over at her owners with an air of quiet triumph and totters off down the stairs.

* * *

It is early evening and Jess and the two girls are sitting in the garden of 42 Chestnut Drive under the Copper Beech, while Marge sets the folding table and Tony bustles about in the kitchen preparing the dinner. Chekhov is under the table. She can smell fish in the air.

Jess is sitting on a green garden chair writing in a notebook. She is writing about cats.

> *'Cats are rather like therapists. They give you unconditional positive regard, are acutely observant and have infinite curiosity. Yet you have no idea at all about what they get up to most of the time.'*

'What are you doing, love?' says Marge.

'Writing a story,' says Jess.

'Oooh lovely! What's it about?' asks Marge.

'Well it's a comedy. About cats... and a rather eccentric couple in Lockdown... David and Linda. Just a silly thing.'

'Sounds wonderful!' says Marge. 'Can I read it?'

THE FISH WON'T WAIT!

'Yes Mom, when it's finished!'

'Are you all ready? The fish is nearly done!' calls Tony from the kitchen.

'Yes, we're all here,' calls Marge.

A loud peeping noise indicates the arrival of the fish. Tony appears in his apron holding a large frying pan full of fried fish in one hand a spatula in the other.

'Oooh lovely,' says Marge.

'Well done Dad,' says Jess.

'I'm vegetarian,' says Rowan.

Tony freezes. 'Oh God!!!!! A vegetarian? A VEGETARIAN? How is a chef supposed to cope?' he says with a dramatic pathos worthy of Macbeth.

'The planet needs saving,' says Rowan.

'I need saving!' mutters Tony.

'Join the Rebellion Grandad!'.

'Let's have some wine,' says Marge picking up the bottle. 'What is it Tony?'

'It's a very nice …... Apassimento... sun ripened grapes…my favourite.'

They tuck into their fish, (except Rowan) followed by salad with beetroot and grapes and a broad bean garlic dip with homemade bread. Next is the Freekeh with a black lentil salad, pheasant with braised cabbage and mustard seed dressing on the side, buttered potatoes and a rich wine sauce. Tony has produced a fried egg for Rowan.

It is all very splendid.

'My favourite,' says Marge. 'You are clever Tony!'

'This is very nice Dad,' says Jess. 'And I did well for buying it all!'

'Yes Jess, you are a very good shopper!'

'Very nice Grandad,' says Ada.

'I like the egg,' says Rowan.

Marge slips a little fish under the table for Chekhov who gobbles it up with relish.

* * *

PC Patel drives slowly down Chestnut Drive ready for his lunch. He stops as usual outside number 42 and peers up the drive. Sure as anything there is the prize waiting on the step. These are the best samosas he's ever eaten. Beats anything his mom ever made, although he wouldn't tell her that. He steps out of the car and checks that no-one is around. The coast is clear. Up he goes, picks a couple of nice big ones and heads back to the patrol car. Perfect.

Week 4

Marge watches the evening news with a certain amount of gloom. Even Chekhov is looking miserable.

'Lockdown restrictions in the UK will continue for "*at least*" another three weeks as it tackles the coronavirus outbreak,' Dominic Raab has said.

The Foreign Secretary told the daily No 10 briefing that a review had concluded relaxing the measures now would risk harming public health and the economy.

'We still don't have the infection rate down as far as we need to,' he said.

It comes as the UK recorded another 861 coronavirus deaths in hospital, taking the total to 13,729.'

Marge takes a large swig of Campari.

Upstairs on the landing, the grandfather clock is chiming into the shadows. For whom does the bell toll tonight?
'Bong... bong... bong...'

* * *

It is late morning. The newts are gently basking just under the surface of the pond. A hot sun rides high in the sky above the Copper Beech. The leaves have now opened and shed a coppery glow in the warm sunshine. A pair of squirrels chase up the trunk. Tony and Marge are sitting in the garden on folding green garden chairs, drinking cups of coffee. Tony has the Financial Times weekend newspaper on his lap. Marge is reading this month's BMJ. It is very warm and she is wearing her long summer skirt and wicker bonnet with a spray of plastic flowers around the rim. Chekhov is sitting underneath Tony's chair sensibly in the shade.

'What day is it today?' asks Marge.

'No idea,' replies Tony.

'I suppose it doesn't matter. Nothing happens. Nobody comes. Nobody goes. It's all the same, all the same...' comments Marge wistfully.

'Hmmm,' replies Tony.

'You never listen Tony!'

'I am listening!'

'Well what did I say then?'

'I dunno. Something about it's all the same. What's all the same?'

'It doesn't matter.'

'Go on tell me Marge. I want to know now. Have you been reading the Daily Mail again?' Tony looks up from his paper.

'Everything. Everything is the same. We get up, we drink coffee, we read the paper, we tidy up...'

'I tidy up,' mutters Tony.

'I talk to patients, I make phone calls, I make notes...'

'Yes, that's a pity,' mutters Tony under his breath.

'We eat lunch, you write your book, we watch the news, you cook dinner, we eat dinner...'

'We drink wine...'

'Yes we drink wine...'

'Very good wine I should add...'

'Yes, alright Tony... we drink very good wine...'

'We watch TV and then we go to bed. Then we start again the next day just the same.'

'That's the routine of life Marge. We are creatures of the earth.'

'The routine of life?'

'Sounds perfect to me, Marge. Couldn't be better.'

'I dunno Tony. What's the point of it all? Really?'

'The point is... there is no point. Why does there have to be a point?' Tony laughs.

'Well there must be a point.'

'Why? We are born, we potter about for a bit and then we die. Go back to where we came from. That's all there is. Poof and we're gone. Gone and forgotten,' says Tony matter of factly. 'Listen to Spinoza, *the more you struggle to live, the less you live. Give up the notion that you must be sure of what you are doing. Instead, surrender to what is real within you*'.

'There should be a point, Tony. There must be something else.'

'Time for you to go back to church Marge. Hark! I can hear God calling...'

'I can't, it's closed. The doors to God's house are firmly closed.'

'The sinners repent!!...'

'Speak for yourself!'

'The plague is upon us!' Tony shakes the Financial Times dramatically.

'Well it's all online now. I just watched the Bishop

doing the sermon from his kitchen on Youtube.'

'Sounds very dull.'

'No, he had a lovely kitchen, all natural wood and brass fittings. A very nice looking Gaggia coffee machine. You would like that Tony.'

'Well you can get me that for my birthday... if the Bishop's got one it must be good. I wonder if John Lewis has one. Shame it's bloody closed or we could go and have a look.'

'I really miss Barbara, Tony. I really miss our trips out shopping...'Marge looks forlorn.

'Don't worry my love, things will all sort out. You'll see. Listen to Spinoza, '*there is no hope unmingled with fear and no fear unmingled with hope*'.

'I hope so Tony. I really hope so.'

'There's always things to do. Lists to make.'

'Yes Tony. Always things to do.'

There is a knock at the side gate and Avni the neighbour from opposite pops her head round.

'Hello, Marge are you there?'

'Oh hello Avni! Lovely to see you, do come in. Find a chair and sit down...'

'Well, I won't stay, but I was wondering if you'd like me to help you with some gardening? I noticed the brambles are getting very long at the front...'

"Well' said Marge, 'That would be very kind if you don't mind.'

'No problem at all. I'll pop back later and we can make a start.'

'Lovely okay, see you later on then! Bring some gloves!!'

Avni heads off back through the gate.

'Well that's nice of Avni. See people do care!'

'Foolish if you ask me!'

'People are kind.'

'That may be so. I like it on my own. I don't want bothering. People are such botherers.'

'Well it's only Avni. We'll keep very quiet.'

'Let's go Marge. Let's just go!' Tony sits up abruptly.

'Yes! Let's go! Where?' Marge brightens up suddenly.

'Anywhere! Name a place Marge and we'll go!'

'Torquay!'

'Torquay? Really Marge is that the best you can think of?'

'No…no….The Outer Hebrides!'

'YES! We can see puffins and listen to whales!' Tony is getting very animated.

'And whisky Tony! We can drink some fine Scottish whisky!'

'And the sea and the sky Marge! So free. So free... we'll be free Marge... we can have long walks and fine dinners… and spend the nights on the beach looking at the stars…and there won't be any people... no people to bother us... Let's get our things…let's get ready right now!' Tony folds up the paper and stands up.

Marge ponders for a moment. 'We can't Tony. It's Lockdown.' she says quietly.

'Oh. Oh yes. Yes, you're right. It's bloody Lockdown.' Tony frowns and sits down again in his chair.

'Well, that's it then,' says Marge sadly.

'That's it then.'

'Read your paper Tony, I've got a meeting now.'

'Ok well. There's a good bit here about Keir Starmer. That'll pass the time.'

'Oh lovely, Tone! Listen out for the knock, I expect our lunch will arrive soon.'

Marge goes in to start her meeting.

* * *

Later that afternoon.

Marge is sitting at the dining room table on a Zoom call to work. Tony is slouched in the darkened lounge writing his book. They had a lovely lunch of vegetable dhal and samosas left on the doorstep by Riya.

The phone rings. After several minutes of ringing it stops. The phone rings again.

Tony hoists himself ungainly out of the sofa and heads to the kitchen to answer the phone.

It stops just as he reaches it.

'Bugger it!!' says Tony heading back to the lounge.

The phone rings again.

'Why can't people leave me alone? This blasted phone!!' This time Tony manages to pick it up.

"Hello?' he says in a rather annoyed tone.

'Yes…Yes this is Tony. You're what? NHS? Volunteer are you?... how am I? ... Yes well you know... not the easiest situation... got to carry on you know... surrounded by bloody papers... it's all such a mess... I can't get any peace and quiet... phone always ringing... at least the weather is nice... yes... shopping?... Well actually that would be very useful…yes…some wine would be very good... two bottles of Villa Vincini if they have it on offer... actually get six of you can. And we're running low on Campari. Get a couple of bottles. That would be fantastic... yes thanks a lot. You've got the address?... yes okay bye.'

Tony heads back to the sofa in a much lighter mood.

'Tick... tick... tick,' sings the grandfather clock with a playful air. Tick, tock goes the clock, and now what shall we play?

* * *

It is late afternoon and Marge and Avni are in the garden cutting the ivy and brambles around the pond. Marge is wearing large gardening gloves and her wicker hat. Avni is wearing a floppy hat which has a sun shield flap at the back. She heaves great clumps of ivy into a wheelbarrow which, when full up, she wheels to the Back Land and dumps onto a pile. Tony is sitting in his writing hut working on his book. It is beautiful warm weather.

'Gosh there is so much of this awful ivy, it just climbs everywhere!' says Marge.

'Yes it's awful isn't it,' replies Avni. 'We just have to keep going Marge; we'll get it all off eventually.'

'Yes, I expect so' puffs Marge, feeling rather tired. Avni has so much energy and Marge is struggling to keep up with her.

'Do you enjoy gardening Avni?' asks Marge.

'Yes, it really helps me to come here. Actually it's good to get out of the house,' replies Avni.

'Oh' says Marge, 'is everything alright?'

'Well, not really Marge. It is all a bit lonely. I've been on my own now for ten years. I feel I'm just rattling round the house. The children live so far away.'

'Oh, I am sorry to hear that Avni. Ten years is a long

time. You're welcome to come round here any time.'

'That's kind of you Marge. Good friends are everything.'

With boundless energy, Avni heaves another load of ivy into the wheelbarrow and begins her trundle up the garden. When she is out of sight, Marge sits down heavily on one of the green garden chairs. She has had enough of gardening for one day and is wondering how she can get out of doing any more.

At that moment Joe and Jeff sweep into the Pinkton driveway in their yellow Volkswagen minivan with a colourful rainbow painted over the words, '*RAINBOW PAWS - making cats happy since 2015*' on one side. They are coming on their regular weekly visit to feed and play with Chekhov.

'You do the photos and I'll play,' says Joe.

'Okay sure, I'll get the camera,' replies Jeff, picking up his impressively large Nikon and hooking it around his neck.

'Have you packed the string and fishy treats?' asks Joe rummaging in a bag on the back seat.

'Yes, they should be there.'

Joe and Jeff let themselves in through the side gate as usual and head into the back garden to look for Chekhov. Chekhov is a shrewd and cunning animal who usually keeps mainly to herself, but she does have a particular weakness for fishy treats and string. Luckily Joe and Jeff have plenty of them.

Jeff positions himself on the lawn with his camera while Joe sets about looking for the cat who is currently nowhere to be seen. They don't notice Marge who is sitting on the other side of the pond.

'Princess!! Where are you my darling?' calls Joe softly. 'Come to Daddy!! Where are you my Princess?'

There is no sign of the cat so Joe crawls under the bushes which he knows is a particularly popular hiding spot.

'Where are you my Princess? Come to me darling!'

Marge, who is sitting on the other side of the pond pricks up her ears.

'Tony? Is that you?'

'Where are you my Princess?' coaxes Joe in his soft voice.

Marge feels a slight warmth rising to her cheeks. This is unusual. Tony isn't usually this demonstrative, especially at this time in the afternoon. And Avni will be back with the wheelbarrow at any moment.

'Princess!! My darling Princess!!' calls Joe slightly louder crawling deeper into the bush. 'Where are you?'

Marge cannot resist any longer. She gets up and inspects the bush from where she can hear the voice eminating.

'Tony are you in there?' She peers through her thick glasses into the deep shadows.

'Come to Daddy Princess!' calls Joe, 'I've got some fishy treats!'

Fishy treats? Marge is perplexed. Why would Tony have fishy treats? She gets on her hands and knees and crawls carefully into the bush. A low twig knocks her hat off and scratches her slightly on the forehead.

'I'm coming my Prince!' she calls. Marge is getting rather excited. This is all rather thrilling! A scene from her favourite opera, The Marriage of Figaro, pops into her head. She imagines herself as Suzanna in the garden scene in Act four, being pursued by her lover Figaro. Her glasses have now fallen off and everything is rather a blur.

'Would you like a game of string my darling? I know how you like your string...'calls Joe.

String? Why would she like string? This is a whole new side to Tony she knew nothing about...

'Where are you my Prince?' she calls again.

Joe stops dead in his tracks. The blood drains from his face. What was that? In all his years as a cat sitter he's never known one to speak before.

'Where are you my Prince?'

In a panic, Joe crawls hastily backwards out of the bush and crashes into Jeff who is poised ready for a photo on the lawn.

'Hey! Watch out, the camera is all set up!' says Jeff angrily.

Joe looks ashen. 'F ... f...f....f...fuck...'he splutters.

Just then Chekhov comes ambling out of the bush ready for a fishy treat and a game of string. Joe's eyes widen and his mouth falls open.

'Now THAT is one HELL of a cat Jeff!!' he says emphatically.

Meanwhile Avni has returned with her empty wheelbarrow and is looking for Marge.

'Marge!! Marge!!' she calls. There is no sign of Marge but there is a strange rustling in the bushes. Avni bends down to investigate and sees Marge's wicker hat hanging off a twig inside the bush. How very odd, she thinks.

'Marge... Marge... are you in there?' she calls. Marge

must have got carried away chopping the ivy.

Marge has become wedged between two low branches and her skirt is all caught up in brambles. She tries to reverse but it's no use. She is stuck.

'Help! Help me I'm stuck!' she cries.

Avni gets down on her hands and knees and plunges head first into the bush.

'I'm coming Marge!'

Half an hour later, Tony is ambling down the lawn, ready for his tea and cake. He comes across a rather unusual scene. The cat is jumping around energetically with two young men on the lawn, one of whom is taking photos with a large camera. Just then he spots two dishevelled forms crawling out from the nearby bush. Could that be Marge and Avni? What on earth? It's hard to tell... they are covered in leaves, twigs and scratches. They look distinctly displeased. Click! Jeff snaps the shutter and captures the moment for eternity.

'I'm ready for my tea,' says Tony hopefully.

* * *

It is late evening and the setting sun, like a golden egg yolk, is sending streaks of red, purple and orange across a pink and yellow sky. Two pigeons are sitting in the Copper Beech preparing to settle for the night. Tony is standing on the front doorstep looking out absently.

'Tony? What are you doing?' asks Marge.

'Oh nothing much. Passing the time.'

'Passing the time...'

'...majestic.'

'Majestic? Oh yes... it is wonderful...'says Marge noticing the sunset. 'Oh Tony! How lovely, you're admiring the sunset! Yes it is really majestic! You're an old romantic!'

She takes his hand in hers.

'Yes majestic,' repeats Tony, gazing intently down the driveway.

'Makes you feel so small and insignificant doesn't it. There's a bigger world out there Tony. Bigger than us all. It's wonderful…when you think about that all your problems seem so small and pointless. What does it all mean in the end? The world goes on and on all on its own...'

A white Ford van swerves into the driveway.

'Oh, here they are. Excellent!' says Tony striding forward. On the side of the van is a logo which reads 'MAJESTIC WINES.'

'See, just on time, Marge, the wine has arrived! Marvellous!'

* * *

Chekhov is hiding in her special spot deep in the bush by the pond. She is watching a large spider tread carefully across the dead leaves. Suddenly it stops... pauses... then pounces on an unsuspecting woodlouse, wrapping it tight in its long legs. Chekhov hears a noise... it's coming from the pond. She turns her head to see flashes of light. Creeping nearer she is amazed to see great flashes of colour... all the colours of the rainbow... rising and falling in the sunlight. Then she realises. They are fish! Huge, marvellous fish jumping and splashing... leaping and thrashing up out of the water, dazzling in the light, then plunging back down with a tremendous splash. Chekhov watches entranced... amazed... intoxicated...

'Chekhov!' calls a familiar voice. 'Fish time!'

It's fish time! She rushes over to the kitchen door. On her plate is the most beautiful fish she has ever seen. Chekhov brings her nose close to savour the aroma. She opens her mouth for the first bite...

Chekhov opens her eyes. It is dark and quiet. Where's the fish? She sniffs. Oh. Oh no! She's in her usual spot. On Tony's chest. How disappointing. Must be night time. She settles back down. Oh well. Maybe there'll be some nice fish tomorrow.

Week 5

The wheel of life is slowly turning. The coot in the park has found herself mother to 6 tiny babies. The daddy coot is exhausting himself with the constant feeding jobs. The swans have 2 cignets, the geese have various goslings following them around obediently and there are 3 new grebe offspring. They cheep loudly and incessantly for food. A common annoyance that all parents of whatever physical form can readily identify with.

* * *

Marge finds herself taking part in a cat quiz organised on Zoom by Joe and Jeff from 'Rainbow Paws'. She didn't mean to be there but accidentally pressed 'join' on the email which then automatically linked her to the event. Once she was in she felt obliged to continue, everyone looked so happy to see her. Besides, Joe and Jeff are devoted cat sitters to Chekhov and Marge feels she should do her bit to support them. Marge could see about 10 faces all lined up in neat rows, a bit like that programme University Challenge. She recognises Tina from down the road and waves at her. Tina waves back, as do all the other cat owners on the screen.

'Ok, question number one. What's a cat breed native to Scotland?' asks Jeff.

Marge has no idea. 'TONY…TONY… WHAT'S A BREED OF CAT NATIVE TO SCOTLAND?' she shouts to Tony who is cooking in the kitchen.

'WHAT?' shouts Tony.

Marge decides to make a guess. 'Persian,' she says.

A contestant named Mr Clipps suggests the Manx cat.

An elderly lady called Joyce's chips in, 'the Scottish Fold Cat is native to Scotland. It is a breed of domestic cat with a natural dominant-gene mutation that affects cartilage throughout the body, causing the ears to 'fold', bending forward and down towards the front of the head, which gives the cat what is often described as an owl-like appearance.'

'Well I didn't know that!' says Marge. Everyone else is looking rather surprised. That Joyce is one to watch.

'That's one point to Joyce. Well done Joyce!' says Joe.

'Next question,' says Jeff. 'On October, 18th, 1963 Felicette, also known as 'Astrocat' was the first and only cat to do what?'

A few ideas come in: 'fly with wings' … 'shoot out of a cannon'…'parashoot.'

'Fly in a hot air balloon,' suggests Marge.

'I know the answer' says Joyce. Everyone's heart sinks.

'Go on then Joyce,' says Jeff.

'Felicette otherwise known as 'Astrocat' was the first and only cat to go into space,' says Joyce.

'Well done, that's another point to Joyce,' says Jeff.

WEEK 5

Marge is starting to think this quiz has been rigged. Who is this Joyce anyway? The prize is a month's supply of cat food and that would be very useful. Marge must work out a strategy.

'TONY!!! TONY!!!' she calls loudly. 'I NEED HELP!!' There is no answer.

'Next question,' says Joe. 'Are you ready?'

There is a frenzy of nodding heads lined up in neat rows. There is an unspoken feeling in the air. A palpable tension. Someone must beat Joyce.

'A house cat is what percentage tiger?' asks Joe. 'Nearest guess wins.'

'67%' says Mrs Drone.

'89%' says Marge.

'45%' says Mr Clipps.

'95.6% says Joyce.

'47%' says Betty.

'Okay, okay... good guesses everybody. And the right answer is 95.6%. Well done Joyce!'

Everyone starts to boo and hiss. There is cheating going on here, Marge is sure of it.

'Next question' says Jeff. 'Okay here we go... which famous scientist invented the cat door?'

'Einstein,' says Betty.

'Louis Pasture,' says Marge.

'Isaac Newton,' says Joyce.

'Yes! Joyce wins again- it was Isaac Newton!'

All at once everyone spots a small boy jump up and down next to Joyce.

'Get down Johnny!' says Joyce poking him back under the table.

'But we got it right!' shouts Johnny. 'I told you

Google knows everything Grandma!'

Joyce's face turns the colour of beetroot. She has been rumbled.

'Cheat... cheat... cheat... cheat...'chant the others.

'Now now everybody!' says Jeff, 'calm down!'

'CHEAT... CHEAT...CHEAT ...CHEAT...'

'SILENCE!!' orders Jeff sternly. 'I hereby declare that Joyce is disqualified for cheating and we will have a re-run of the quiz again next week.'

Marge switches off the computer with a triumphal smile. 'That was great!!'

Joe and Jeff heave a long sigh of relief. Thank goodness that was on Zoom. In real life that could have ended in violence.

'I'll get us a gin and tonic,' says Jeff.

'Make mine a large one,' says Joe reaching down for a soothing cuddle with Edna.

* * *

Great piles of rubbish are collecting outside 42 Chestnut Drive. Tony and Marge have forgotten to put the bins out for 3 weeks in a row. It is a problem when everyday is more or less the same. The days just roll on... days of the week become meaningless. Unless of course there is rubbish to put out.

* * *

Tony is in a small white square room. It is empty except for a small cat flap in one corner. He is sitting on the cold white floor trying to set a timer for 2 minutes 30 seconds.

But something is wrong... it's broken. Suddenly the cat comes through the flap, walks over, sits down and starts to lick her paws. Tony looks up and notices that above is a blue sky with fluffy white clouds. Suddenly it grows dark and the clouds draw in. Snow starts to fall, thick and fast. Chekhov rushes out through the cat flap. Then Tony notices it's not snow at all... it looks like papers, papers with scrawly handwriting on, falling down on top of him. The floor is now thick with papers, but they keep on coming, more and more until he is entirely covered. He feels the weight of them on his chest, he cannot breathe... no... no... !!! The timer goes off and fills the room with deafening beeps. Beep beep…beep beep…beep beep…Clawing away at the papers, Tony crawls over to the cat flap and tries to push his head through, but the opening is too small. 'Let me out!' cries Tony pressing his head hard against the cat flap.

'Let me out!!!! LET ME OUUUUUUTTTTTT!!!'

Nothing can be done. Darkness takes over...

Tony sits up in bed gasping and spluttering. Chekhov, who a minute ago was sleeping peacefully on top of Tony's chest, jumps off in alarm. Blast that wretched cat! Tony looks at his watch - then remembers it's broken. What time is it? He gets out of bed, opens the curtains and looks outside. It's dark. An orange moon looks back at Tony with its watery eye. Must be night time. Has he put the rubbish out? Where is Marge? There is a lump in the bed. Good. Tony gets back into bed. He closes his eyes. Think of something nice... a nice ice cream on the beach... a strawberry ice cream in a cone... with sprinkles on top …mmmm…

THE FISH WON'T WAIT!

'Bong... bong... bong,' goes the distant chime of the grandfather clock. Old Father Time.

* * *

Edna is sitting in her bath. She loves her bath. Jeff pours in the cat shampoo and it bubbles up into white puffs of sweet scented froth.

'Does that feel nice?' croons Joe, splashing warm froth over her back.

Edna closes her big olive green eyes and purrs loudly and happily.

'Who's a gorgeous girl then?' says Jeff, massaging shampoo onto her bald head and around her large bat-like ears.

Edna pads at a small yellow duck bobbing in the foam. Finally it is time to come out. Jeff holds up a warmed fluffy towel and Joe gently lifts Edna out of the bath into the towel wrapping her up tightly.

'Oooh there's a good girl, nice and dry,' says Joe rubbing her gently.

Her bald face peering out of the towel gives her the appearance of E.T. But that doesn't matter. She feels like a real goddess.

Jeff chooses a pink hooded towelling fleece with the words 'GIRL POWER' branded on the front in Swarovsky crystals. Together they slip it over her head. Next, four little white knitted leg warmers pop on and she's all done.

'I've got something special for you,' smiles Joe reaching into his pocket.

Edna knows exactly what will come next and she fixes

her big eyes on Joe expectantly.

'A fishy treat!!' Pure and utter bliss.

Time for a gin and tonic.

* * *

Tony and Marge are in the kitchen. Tony is rummaging in his box of vegetables. Marge is unloading the dishwasher.

'You see this Marge... it's a wonderful thing!' Tony picks a small white and mauve vegetable with sprouting green leaves, out of the box and holds it up.

'What is it Tony?'

'This is a turnip!' says Tony proudly. 'Turnips are wonderful things!'

'Really Tony? Can I have a look?'

Tony passes the turnip to Marge.

'Well it does look rather nice...'says Marge with a slight skepticism. To her, vegetables all look rather the same. But in different colours.

'People don't rate turnips but they have a fantastic taste.'

'Gosh,' says Marge giving it a sniff.

'I'll make a fine stew with this and you can see for yourself Marge.'

'How wonderful Tony, I'll look forward to that! Can you put some carrots in it as well?'

'I can if you want...'

'They are good for my eyes.'

'Yes okay.' Tony looks in the box and pulls out a carrot.

'Here, yes I've got carrots.' He passes one to Marge.

She looks carefully at the turnip in one hand and the carrot in the other.

'Wonderful things vegetables,' says Tony.

'Very wonderful Tone,' says Marge emphatically. 'I know, I'll ask Cap to grow some turnips on the Back Land!'

'Excellent idea! He will enjoy that!' says Tony.

Week 6

Tennessee Tim is inspecting himself closely in a long mirror in the largest bedroom of his 1930's semi detached house in Smethwick. He is wondering whether to go for the white sequinned cape or the red one with the American Eagle. He checks the clock. He has ten minutes to set up before the Thursday clapping starts. Every Thursday Tennessee Tim performs his Elvis routine on the front lawn to entertain the locals and raise money for the NHS.

It has become an event that 83 year old Gladys, two doors away at number 67, eagerly looks forward to. As she is vulnerable and shielding, it is the only time she comes out of the house. It is, in fact, the highlight of her week. At five minutes to eight precisely she opens the front door, hobbles down the path in her dressing gown and slippers. She stands holding the gate with one hand and a large sherry with the other. Around her neck a red nylon scarf that Tim gave her a few weeks back, wafts in the breeze. It has the logo 'Tennessee Tim', a phone number and a small silhouette of Elvis printed on one side.

Opposite, at number 87 lives 92 year old Ernie and his wife Doris. Out he comes, wheeling Doris in her wheel chair. Ernie and Doris are also wearing red scarves. Almost all the residents of Woody Crescent are out by eight and as the clapping starts, Tennessee Tim launches passionately into 'Hound Dog' at full force.

This week Tim is wearing his fabulous white jump suit with the gold sequins and red Eagle cape. His costumes are devotedly designed and hand made by his Mother-in-law and manager who spends long evenings attaching sequins in front of the TV. She can almost get half a leg done in an episode of Coronation Street. His greased, jet black hair is slicked back and his stick on sideburns are placed with absolute precision. For fifteen minutes the entire road comes alive to the heady sounds of Elvis, pulsing, grinding and heaving into the evening air. *Hound Dog* is followed by *All Shook Up, Suspicious Minds, Fever, Are you Lonesome Tonight* and then finally, Gladys's favourite, *Love me Tender*. As the soft deep tones waft along the street, Gladys is transported back to a happier time, back to 1957 when she first met Frank at the church fete and they danced long into the night. She sways softly and you can just hear her thin, rasping whisper whistling through her plastic teeth… *'love me tender, love me true all my dreams fulfill…for my darlin', I love you, and I always will…'*

* * *

It is Jess's birthday this month and Marge and Tony are planning a small party to celebrate.

Tony has spent many long hours planning the cuisine. He has found an excellent fish recipe in last week's Financial Times, a whole salmon poached in Middle Eastern spices and lentils with bulgar wheat and fresh herbs. He has found an interesting vegetarian recipe for spiced aubergine frittatas which will be fine for Rowan. A case of fine wine will be arriving from Majestic and all he needs to do now is sort out the dessert.

* * *

PC Patel has been sitting in his patrol car under the bush at Muggin's park for the past three hours. He has counted 23 squirrels, 34 pigeons, 8 coots, 14 baby coots, 14 moorhens, 5 swans, 3 cygnets and estimates more than 300 Canada geese. Most of those geese are now surrounding his patrol car as he has just thrown yesterday's egg sandwich out of the window. Two geese are now on top of the car, one is pecking the windscreen. His mom makes him an egg sandwich for lunch everyday. He is utterly sick of egg sandwiches. Luckily he has found a new lunch opportunity. He looks at his watch. Mmmm another half an hour and he'll set off. To 42 Chestnut Drive.

* * *

It is late morning. Priscilla is sitting on Tennessee Tim's kingsize bed licking her nether regions. She is a truly glorious creature. Watery pale blue eyes, a perfect pink nose and glossy thick white fur. Around her neck is a velvet red collar studded with tiny white crystals and a TCB logo in gold hangs at the front. She is Tim's pride and joy.

This morning, Tennessee Tim is sitting in bed next to Priscilla reading his latest purchase, '*Elvis, What Happened?*' He is wearing his dark blue satin pyjamas. It is

10.35am but there's nothing much to get up for today. His gig tonight at the local golf club was cancelled due to the 'situation'. In fact all his gigs this month have been cancelled. He's been posting videos of himself on Facebook, but only had four 'likes' on the last one. He has recently put on six pounds in weight and his jumpsuits are getting rather tight round the middle. The Mother-in-law has had to sew in an extra tummy flap to accommodate. She is very displeased. Tim takes a sip of stale lager from his Elvis mug. This book is pretty dismal. Tim is feeling pretty dismal. He still feels a deep hurt left when the Missus ran off with another 'Elvis' at the New Year 2016 European Elvis Championship. A 1968 Elvis no less, in bloody black leather. What a bastard!

He leans back on his white satin pillow, closes his eyes, lets out a deep sigh and imagines the grim headline on his Facebook page, 'Tennessee Tim... What Happened?'

* * *

It is morning, the dew on the lawn is sparkling and the sun is shining brightly promising a beautiful day. A variety of tits are busy pecking nuts from the bird feeders in Jess's garden. Jess, Rowan and Ada are brewing beer in the kitchen. Beatles music blasts out from the speaker on the table, a constant backdrop to family life. Rowan is a devoted Beatles fan. Kewpie the cat is watching curiously from her spot on the chair. Jess hopes that the heady smell of hops will help Rowan feel more at home.

Unfortunately Jess has accidentally screwed the tap to the barrel on wrongly and now the beer is pouring out all over the floor. The cat is licking up the brown pooling liquid. Oh blimey! *Help!* sings John Lennon,

I need somebody

Help! not just anybody

Help! you know I need someone

Help!

Thinking quickly, they transfer the beer into a variety of pans and bowls. Phew! All is well. In a few days the beer will be ready for bottling. All ready for her birthday!

And now my life has changed in oh so many ways

My independence seems to vanish in the haze

But every now and then I feel so insecure

I know that I just need you like I've never done before...

* * *

Tony makes a cake everyday without fail so the lack of flour has come as rather a heavy blow. Luckily after a bit of research he has found an excellent recipe that replaces flour with All Bran. It is a simple one cup of everything method. He is experimenting using different ingredients such as walnuts, apples and dried fruits. Best of all he is trying seeping the cake in alcohol to add a depth of flavour. Today he is trying whisky.

* * *

Jess has noticed that packets of All Bran and various types of alcohol are appearing on the shopping lists rather more frequently than before. To her delight however, gradually the lists have been improving. They are now written on large sheets of paper in less scrawly handwriting with the items listed in itemised sections. Tony has become very particular about his lists. This is very good news for Jess. It is a truth universally acknowledged that good shopping depends entirely upon a good list.

* * *

'Come back Cilla!! I won't give you Whiskas again I promise!!'

Tim is chasing Priscilla through the musical gates and up the curving driveway. He sees her slip up the steps and through the front door left slightly ajar. Tim puffs his way up the steps, pushes the door open and finds himself in an entrance hall. There's no sign of Priscilla. He looks around in amazement. A beautiful white carpet, a stained glass window with a peacock motif. To the left is a dining room. To the right the living room with long white sofas and a soft white carpet. There is a grand piano. He hears sounds of music and laughter coming from another room at the rear. He follows the sounds and finds himself in a darkened room filled with people. It has a green carpet on both floor and ceiling. There is plastic foliage everywhere. It reminds him of a jungle. This must be The Den. Someone hands him a drink. Over in the corner, on an animal skin sofa sits someone in a bright pink short sleeved shirt with ruffles down the front. Tim's knees buckle and his heart is pounding. The figure in pink stands up and strides over towards him.

'Good to see you Son!' The figure puts a warm hand on his shoulder. Tim is speechless.

'I... I…I…' says Tim.

'It's gonna be okay my boy,' says the figure holding him firm with his piercing blue gaze.

'Oh…oh…' Tim can no longer control his emotions and tears come to his eyes.

'It's okay, Son. Everything's gonna be alright...'

'Oh…' says Tim.

'Don't worry 'bout a thing. Cause every little thing gonna be alright.'

That's strange. Tim is sure that reminds him of something.

The room swells into music and the figure in pink leads the gathering in a song,

'Three little birds

Pitch by my doorstep

Singin' sweet songs

Of melodies pure and true

Saying, this is my message to you

THE FISH WON'T WAIT!

Singing' don't worry 'bout a thing

'Cause every little thing gonna be alright

Singing' don't worry 'bout a thing

'Cause every little thing gonna be alright.'

Tim opens his eyes. Priscilla is sleeping on the pillow next to him. His body is covered in a film of cold sweat. He has the feeling that something awesome has just happened. Something tremendous. A song pops into his head. It's not by Elvis, but that doesn't matter. Someone cares for him. He felt it. He feels it still. For sure.

* * *

Marge has been wandering about in the house for about half an hour looking for her hat. She has looked everywhere but it is nowhere to be found.

In the cupboard... under the stairs... on the sofa... on the table... in the bathroom... in the kitchen... under the papers...

'TONY!' she calls from the kitchen.

'WHAT?' calls back Tony from the living room.

'HAVE YOU SEEN MY HAT?'

'OH GOD NOT AGAIN!'

'I HAD IT YESTERDAY ON THE WALK.'

'DID YOU PUT IT IN THE BAG WITH THE CHEESE?'

'I DON"T KNOW. WHERE IS THE BAG WITH THE CHEESE?'

WEEK 6

'IN THE FRIDGE.'

Marge opens the fridge and searches for the bag with the cheese. There it is at the bottom. She opens the bag and sure enough there is her hat, an umbrella and a nice piece of cheese.

She pops it on. It's a bit cold and smells of Camembert, but no matter. At least it lives to see another day.

* * *

PC Patel is sitting in his patrol car under the bush at Muggins Park. It is a beautiful warm day and he has the music on loud. He taps his fingers to the heavy beats of Stormzy. He has a dry egg sandwich on his lap and a coffee filled flask. Suddenly he spots an unusually large goose swimming on the lake. Eh?? What?? PC Patel gets out his binoculars for a closer look. It is a goose of truly monstrous size! PC Patel quickly steps out of the car and stands at the waters edge. What the…?

Now the goose is coming towards him... moving fast... skimming across the lake like a giant feathered speed boat. It seems to be fixing its huge beady eyes in his direction. This doesn't look good. Not good at all! PC Patel is hit by a wave of panic. He has a stun gun in his jacket and his hand reaches in towards it. He starts to run... run away as fast as he can... his legs pounding and pounding. He turns. The goose is now heaving with huge powerful legs towards him... catching up... faster and faster... wings outstretched...

PC Patel feels something grip tightly around his waist and the air press out of his lungs as his body lifts up off the ground. He is caught in the gargantuan beak of this monstrous creature, like an ornithological re-make of King Kong. The goose flicks him up high into the air like an unfortunate caterpillar. PC Patel has a brief glimpse of the lake, the bushes, the sky and the clouds as he twists, turns and spins…over ... and over... and over...

PC Patel opens his eyes with a start. He intakes a sharp breath. Where is that goose? His eyes dart around in panic... what? Oh! he's still in the car. The egg sandwich is on his lap. Slightly squashed, but it's okay. He opens the flask, pours a coffee and downs it in one big gulp. Phew! A few geese are roaming around the car. But that's okay. They're only small. PC Patel gathers himself together. That was a tough morning! He winds down the window and throws out the egg sandwich. It is ripped apart in a violent flurry of beaks and feathers.

It must be time for lunch.

* * *

It is late April. Jess is sitting on the balcony outside her kitchen door overlooking the garden, drinking green tea. She has been writing her story. It is coming on fairly well. The garden is a glory of colour and heavy with the scent of blossom. The lilacs peeping their violet heads over the fence shed a fragrant perfume. In the centre of the garden stands an apple tree heavy with snow white blossoms. A scattering of bluebells cluster round the borders and beds of pale yellow primulas reach their little faces up towards the sun. The cat is poised under Jess's chair observing a small spider as she methodically weaves a tiny net in the balcony railings.

Jess is checking Facebook and has just been watching

WEEK 6

Tennessee Tim's latest video post. She has been a fan since that memorable evening at the golf club. 3 hours, 34 Elvis songs, and 5 pints of best bitter later, he had finally won her heart. Rowan and Ada had also endured this performance. They would later describe the ordeal as 'excruciating'.

He has now raised £128.45 for the NHS. She presses 'like' which gives him a total of 5. Then she has an idea. A crazy but wonderful idea! Maybe…just possibly… he would come and sing for her birthday meal? He can't have many bookings right now and it would add something fun to the proceedings. She can't invite her friends due to the Lockdown. If only Tennessee Tim would come, that would make up for it. That would make up for everything. That would help her get through this awful nightmare. That would make her dreams come true.

She types a message:

Hi Tim,
I am your biggest fan. I am having a small birthday garden gathering and I was wondering if you would be able to sing for me?

Thanks,
Jess.

* * *

Jeff, Joe and Edna are sitting up at the kitchen table. It is dinner time and they are enjoying a tasty roast chicken with assorted vegetables. Edna is sitting in her high chair wearing a plastic bib with the words, 'FEED ME' written in big letters along the front. Joe is cutting up a nice piece of chicken breast into small pieces on a 'Hello Kitty' plastic dish. Edna watches him intently with her olive green eyes. Jeff takes the gravy jug and pours a little over the chicken.

'There you go!' says Joe putting the plate in front of Edna. She attacks the chicken greedily and after twenty seconds of noisy gobbling it's all gone. She raises hopeful olive eyes to Joe.

'No more!' says Jeff. 'She's getting fat!'

'No she's not!' says Joe. 'Poor darling... you didn't hear that did you?'

Joe and Jeff tuck into their dinner. It's a lovely moist chicken, Jeff is a great cook. Finally pudding is served. Chocolate mousse (a great Mary Berry recipe) for Joe and Jeff and a special one for Edna.

Sprat mousse! Delicious!

* * *

'Tick... tick... tick ' goes the grandfather clock with a certain agitation. Time is going nowhere.

Tony and Marge have been struggling at the computer all morning. They are trying to upload Microsoft Teams onto Marge's computer for her meetings. It is not working. Now the whole computer has gone blank. It is a disaster. Tensions are frayed. Tony is on the phone to the 'Apple Man' who is trying to sort it out. Marge is pacing up and down frantically in her bed socks.

What will happen if she loses everything? All her work? Her notes? Her emails? Her CPD? All her precious things? It doesn't bear thinking about.

Tony is prodding hopefully at random keys. The screen remains blank and lifeless.

'Oh dear,' says Tony to the man on the phone. 'That's bad news.'

Marge groans loudly.

'Marge, do you remember your password?'

'Well, I wrote it down somewhere...'says Marge. Her heart sinks as she looks at a large pile of papers on the floor.

'Oh dear. Well let's try out a few ideas,' says Tony.

Tony and Marge spend the next thirty minutes trying out various possible password ideas, but none of them work.

Finally at the point of giving up, Tony types in the words, 'Fishy-treats'.

It works!

IT WORKS!!! The screen pops into life and all Marge's emails are intact. What a relief!

'Saved by the cat!' says Tony with more than slight sarcasm.

'Where is she?...I'll get her a treat.' says Marge.

'Excuse me... it's me that deserves the treat!' says Tony sharply.

'Of course you do, Tone you are marvellous!' says Marge stroking his hair.

'Shall I get you a fishy treat?'

'A fishy treat?? I'm not a bloody cat!' says Tony with emphasis.

'Well then, I'll get you a nice biscuit!'

* * *

Priscilla is sitting on the kitchen table watching Tennessee Tim open a tin of Sheba and scrape it slowly into a little bowl. She jumps down off the table and rubs herself against his leg. Her excitement can hardly be contained. There is a scent of rancid old fish in the air. Cod and prawn. It is Priscilla's favourite and the very thought of it is making her drool.

'Miaowwww,' she says. Why is he taking so long?

'Here we go, Cilla,' says Tim finally putting the bowl down on her dinner mat.

Priscilla runs over to the bowl and scoffs it down noisily.

Tim is feeling worried. If he doesn't get a booking soon he won't be able to afford to carry on like this. He will have to cut back and save money. He won't be able to afford Sheba anymore and Cilla hates Whiskas. One sniff of the stuff and it sends her running. If only he could get a booking. All he wants is to keep Priscilla in the lifestyle she deserves.

Tim opens his laptop on the kitchen table and flicks onto his Facebook page. What's this? He's got a message... someone wants to book him... a garden party... a birthday...

Tim takes a deep breath. He can hardly believe it! He has a booking! At last! He can feel his heart thumping under his ribs. A wave of emotion hits him hard. He leans back in his chair and his watery eyes reach up to a large framed picture of Elvis on the wall. Elvis is in Hawaii and is wearing a flowery red shirt with a leis of flowers around his neck. He is strumming a small ukulele.

'Thank you... thank you...' he mutters to the picture. 'I won't let you down... I promise.'

Tim is resolved. This will be the best performance of his life.

* * *

It was a particularly difficult morning on Zoom for Jess with her learners, who are struggling with the Lockdown. Some have suffered the loss of relatives to Covid. Jess is now at the Esso station getting petrol.

'Hey Babes!' says Marv from behind the perspex screen. He is wearing a white face mask.

'God I hate this thing, I can't breathe. I'm always so hot anyway and this is making it worse.'

It must be bad. Jess had never heard Marv moan before.

'It's not all bad,' he laughs, 'at least you can't see my face hahaha!! You know the saying, three things cannot be long hidden - the sun, the moon and the truth.'

'Cool!' says Jess.

'No hot!' laughs Marv, fanning his sweating face which is almost the colour of his Esso top.

'Well, I really hope things get back to normal soon,' says Jess.

'Don't be worryin' bout it. You just carry on what you're doing. Every single one of us is in this together. Like the sun shines everywhere, no matter where you are, what country you're in. Everyday the sunrise gives us hope.'

Marv pulls out a large bag from under the counter. It is his precious bag of crystals. He rummages through it and pulls out a small pinkish one.

'Here, this is for you. It's a rose quartz. It speaks directly to the *Heart Chakra*, dissolving emotional wounds, fears and resentments, and circulates a divine loving energy throughout the entire aura.'

'Gosh!' says Jess.

'Basically it'll help you to feel calm.'

'Wow, that's nice, Marv. Thank you!' Jess pays for her KitKat.

She walks out to the car clutching her crystal. Over the tannoy comes a voice.

'Hey Babes! Ya' know, everything that has a beginning has an ending. Make your peace with that and all will be well.'

Good old Marv.

Evening

Jess has come downstairs to find that the girls have been experimenting with their hair. Ada, who just an hour ago had long flowing locks now has a buzz cut. Rowan has shaved it all off for her with the electric hair clippers. Clumps of hair lie on the balcony slabs outside. Rowan is in the process of dyeing sections of her dark brown hair blonde. It looks rather cool.

'I'm going to dye it green,' says Ada.

* * *

Tony is sitting in the writing hut on the Back Land. He has the laptop on his knees and his fingers are tapping ferociously on the keyboard. The sun is shining and a peacock butterfly is flitting around the window pane hoping to find a way out.

WEEK 6

Suddenly a dark shape creeps across the window casting a deep shadow. Tony carries on typing. Outside the hut, strange things are happening. Ivy, brambles and creepers are starting to move, slithering like snakes, growing longer and longer... winding around the hut... twisting and turning... wrapping and knotting. Now it is dark inside the hut and Tony looks up from his work. What on earth? Tony's eyes widen. What's going on? Is it night time already?

Now the creepers are finding a way into the hut, reaching under the door and under the window... fronds creeping... crawling... twisting...

'MARGE!! MARGE!!' calls Tony. The laptop falls from his knees and clatters into the floor.

Marge is in the garden wearing her gardening gloves and straw hat. She hears a voice calling and makes her way to the Back Land.

'TONY? IS THAT YOU?' she calls.

'MARGE!! MARGE!! HELP!!' calls Tony with a certain urgency.

'I'M COMING TONY!!' Marge spots the writing hut wrapped in the creepers and ivy. She gets her clippers out of her pocket and starts to clip.

'DON'T WORRY TONY! I'M COMING!!' calls Marge.

Now the creepers have reached Tony on his chair. They are winding their way up his trouser legs and pinning him down... wrapping and binding... binding and wrapping...

'MARGE!! I CAN'T MOVE!! HELP!'

Marge is chopping and clipping... and clipping and chopping... when suddenly her phone rings. Oh bother...

who is that? It's the hospital... must be a patient... oh dear! Oh dear! Marge puts the clippers down and peers at the phone.

'MARGE!! HELP!' calls Tony.

Marge stands frozen holding the ringing phone in her hands…she looks and the phone... then she looks at the hut... the phone... the hut... the phone...

The creepers are reaching Tony's throat. He feels the breath squeezing out of his lungs. Now is not the time for indecision.

'MAAARRRRGGGGEE!!!!!'

With the strength of Thor and a mighty swing of her arm, Marge spins the phone high into the air and it disappears deep inside the bush. With the speed of Quicksilver she attacks the creepers, ripping and clipping... clipping and ripping. With the passion of The Hulk, she wrenches the door open. With Herculean power she cuts and chops and chops and cuts, finally extracting Tony from his weedy tethers... just in time.

Marge opens her eyes. Her straw hat has fallen off and she notices she is wearing gardening gloves. She looks round. Avni is wheeling an empty wheel barrow from the Back Land ready for a new load. Oh no! Marge sighs deeply and heaves herself slowly out of the green garden chair. She has surely done enough clipping for one day!

'Come on Marge, the ivy needs cutting!' calls Avni.

* * *

Cap is wiping the sweat from his brow. He is not in a good mood. He has been digging a plot in the Back Land for the past hour and a half. This is a job that he particularly dislikes. It is tedious, involves far too much energy and most crucially takes him away from his beloved mowing. He has been instructed to plant turnips. Cap can't stand turnips. Nasty pasty little creatures. Now an artichoke, well that would be another matter entirely. A whole different ball game. Tall and elegant. Sensual and exotic. The sense of thrill as you unlayer it bit by bit, dipping into the creamy butter, until you reach the soft centre, the secret heart.

But no use daydreaming. Back to the matter in hand. Cap takes the spade, presses it firmly with his boot and it sinks into the soft black ground luckily just missing a small earthworm passing on its way.

* * *

It has been established that every week some of the family come together on Zoom to pitch head to head in a quiz. The role of Quiz Master is taken in turns. These tend to be riotous affairs with questions spanning the heights of art, science and literature and the lows of plague, disease, bodily functions and the fascinating life of slugs. (Fascinating for Jess but nobody else).

Taking part in the UK are Marge, Tony, Jess, Rowan, Ada, Uncle Josh (Jess's brother), Aunty Karen and their children Flossy, Chrissy, Seb, Evie, Ronnie and Jude. The Portugal players consist of Marge's brother Uncle Norm, Aunty Angie and cousin Ria. This week the Quiz Master happens to be Uncle Norm.

This is bad news as his questions are notoriously obscure and aviation related. Uncle Norm is fascinated by aeroplanes, having always wanted to be a pilot. He travelled to Florida specifically to take the flight of his life in 'Crazy Horse', a spectacular P51 Mustang. The feeling as he took the controls was unbelievable. It was his dream come true. Unfortunately not everyone has specific and in-depth knowledge of aviation design and history. The prospect of Norm as Quiz Master fills the party with a certain amount of dread.

'Are you ready?' says Uncle Norm cheerfully. He has been looking forward to this all week. He has spent hours putting together a brilliant selection of questions that spans the full history of world aviation.

'Number 1. Let's start with an easy one. What is the name of the designer of the Spitfire?'

There is a sound of general muttering and whispering.

'Number 2,' says Norm. 'Which aircraft has the current world record for the fastest manned aircraft? You should know this one.'

There are sounds of sighing and groaning.

'Number 3. What plane is also known as the Stealth Bomber, an American heavy strategic bomber, featuring low observable stealth technology designed for penetrating dense anti-aircraft defences?'

There are loud sounds of heavy moaning.

'Can you give us a clue?' says Uncle Josh with a certain desperation. He has a strong competitive streak. Uncle Josh plays to win.

'It has a flying wing design with a crew of two.'

'Humm thanks!' says Uncle Josh. He closes his eyes and reaches into the deepest recesses of his brain. Usually Uncle Josh can pull something useful out of the bag. But on this occasion the landscape is barren. As barren as the Sahara desert during a particularly lengthy heatwave.

Then he remembers Top Gun. What was that plane? Super Wasp... Hornet? That was pretty slick... mmmm... good film...

Ronnie is reaching into his brain and retrieves countless facts about aircraft as a result of many hours of watching Youtube and reading Wikipedia. Just last week he was watching a fascinating video on top US stealth bombers. He knows the answer instantly. It's the Northrop Grumman B-2 Spirit.

Evie is reaching into her brain and proudly remembers the time she won a rosette in a local competition for riding the most attractive older pony. Such a pretty pony.

Instead of reaching into his brain, Seb is asking the cat Jasper, who is sitting next to him on the sofa. In an attempt to help, Jasper takes a brief look into his brain and finds interesting memories of a chewed up mouse and a regurgitated fur ball. Sadly, not too helpful on this occasion.

Marge is also reaching into the deepest recesses of her brain. At this time in the evening it feels rather like stumbling through a haze of dense fog. She is dismayed to find no useful aviation information whatsoever. Suddenly a disturbing memory pops up about the time she got locked in the toilet on a flight to Los Angeles. She remembers banging on the door for a full twenty minutes before she was finally extracted by a very helpful hostess. Tony hadn't even realised she'd gone. Marge quickly blocks that vision with a large gulp of Campari.

'Number 4. Which World War One plane completely changed the face of aerial warfare, with its capacity to dive safely at 249mph being a particular advantage?'

There are sounds of extreme pain.

Tony is reaching into the deepest recesses of his brain. World War One. Tony is fascinated by the Great War generals. He remembers reading an excellent book on Field Marshal Douglas Haig. *'The Butcher of the Somme.'* A controversial character criticised for excessive casualties of British troops under his command on the Western Front. Churchill's postwar debates sparked rage around Haig's reputation for the rest of the twentieth century. One can argue persuasively that Haig did not merely fail in the great battles of the Somme and Ypres. He failed in a much grander sense. Failed classically in the fashion of Pyrrhus, who lamented after the battle at Asculum, *'Another such victory over the Romans and we are undone.'*

Tony pauses in his thoughts. What was the question again?

Jess is also reaching into her brain. World War One. What was that film she saw recently?... 1917... that was incredible... wow... nasty though... that awful scene with all that blood... started to feel dizzy... she had to close her eyes... focus on the popcorn...

Rowan is not reaching deeply into her brain. She is counting on her fingers. She is working out how many more days left until the beer needs bottling.

Ria is also avoiding reaching into her brain and is preoccupied with her phone. She is checking TikTok for the latest interesting lip-sync video.

At six years old, Jude is the youngest member of the party. His brain does not need reaching into. It is a sleek fact machine optimised for dynamic performance, primed with an answer for the toughest questions. Nothing is too challenging or obscure for Jude. His brain has everything at its fingertips. It was the British-built SPAD S.VII of the

WEEK 6

Royal Flying Corps. Easy.

Fifty questions later and the ordeal is over. On this occasion the top score is Ronnie who has twenty points (he has remarkable general knowledge) and the bottom score is Marge and Jess who scored nothing at all.

On the plus side, everyone is much more knowledgeable about aviation. And Uncle Norm has had a wonderful time!

Week 7

It is the day of the party. Tennessee Tim and the Mother-in-law have arrived in their 1950's 'Elvis pink' Morris Minor which is parked in the drive. The Mother-in-law has painted the words '*Tennessee Tim bringing Las Vegas to Smethwick*' in large black and gold letters along one side. She is a woman of many talents. They are setting up their stage area on the lawn. There is a black roll out screen with huge ELVIS letters which light up in red. There is a microphone and speaker system and various lights to hang from a portable scaffold. Luckily the Mother-in-law is very practical and has it all in hand.

Marge is laying the table under a rain canopy, with a large Campari poised in one hand.

Tony is in the kitchen adding the final touches to his salmon. Rachmaninov's 2nd is blasting out from the radio. The lentils are simmering softly in a subtle herb stock. The salmon will take exactly 47 minutes in the oven and must be timed to perfection. He has made a large cake which is steeping in brandy. The homemade bread dough is kneading in the machine, ready in 14 minutes to shape and pop into the oven. All is well. Everything in control. Tony takes a sip of his whisky on ice and wipes his forehead with the oven cloth.

WEEK 7

Riya from next door has provided a vast array of wonderful pakoras, samosas and dosas with chilli sauces. She will pop over later with her two daughters.

Summer is in the air. The garden is heavy with the scent of musk roses, violets and azaleas. Flamingo pink blooms cover the rhododendron bushes and the Back Land is overflowing with wild garlic, cowslips and honeysuckle.

Cap is moving his lawn mower up and down the lawn with unusual force. He is not in a good mood. Firstly Marge has asked him to avoid the daisies. AVOID THE DAISIES??? This is utter madness! His straight and orderly lines will be disrupted by ungainly clumps of those horrid flowers. It will be a disaster. Secondly there are strange people on the lawn disturbing his routine and getting in the way. He is deeply distracted and cannot feel the connection with the Great Mother that he needs for a good cut. This does not bode well.

Chekhov is regarding the scene curiously from her hiding spot deep inside the bush.

There is a loud knock on the door.

'Oh God! What now?' mutters Tony who is at a critical point in the cooking. He wipes his hands on the oven glove and opens the front door. There is a familiar figure on the step. He recognises the large industrial mask and heavy black boots.

'Hajhdahdbdjsblmmmkknnn,' says the fire-man through the mask.

'Hello,' says Tony. 'Good to see you. Come in. You know where to go don't you?'

He ushers the fire-man into the lounge and leaves him to fix the fire. Tony goes back to his cooking.

THE FISH WON'T WAIT!

A steady chime can be heard from upstairs as the grandfather clock swings into action.
'Bong... bong... bong...' We're gonna rock around the clock tonight.

The party has started. An exotic array of food and alcoholic beverages have been set out on the outside table. Tony is still in the kitchen fiddling with the garnishes on his prize fish. Marge's computer is open on a side bench with a grid arrangement of assorted uncles, aunts and cousins on Zoom. They have the distinct disadvantage of not being able to eat the food or drink the copious amounts of alcohol or get a decent view of 'Elvis'. They also have a very limited range of view as Marge accidentally knocked the computer to face the side fence. All they can do is listen to the various goings on with a certain curiosity. Aunty Sue occasionally tries calling out for help, but so far no one has responded.

Riya and her daughters are sitting on the lawn watching the stage gradually taking shape.

Jess is sitting on a green garden chair with a glass of wine in her hand and her notebook on her lap. She is waiting expectantly for Tennessee Tim to appear. About thirty minutes ago he disappeared into the writing hut with his Mother-in-law to get ready and he should be making an appearance very soon. Rowan and Ada are lying on the lawn making daisy chains from the small clumps that Cap has left.

Marge is also sitting on a green chair with her large Campari. This is her third one in the past hour and a half and she is feeling light headed and rather happy. Avni is sitting a sensible distance away with a plateful of food.

'Marge!!!' calls a muffled voice from the computer over by the fence. Nothing happens.

The side gate opens and a new arrival steps cautiously into the garden. It is Greg, Jess's friend from her university days. He has been warned that family parties with her parents tend to be unpredictable and eccentric affairs. He regards the scene with a mixture of caution and curiosity. He side-steps nervously over to Jess and perches on a stone bench near her seat. Jess gets him a beer and he sips it carefully as he surveys the scene. He can see Tony's head from the kitchen window. Delicious smells waft out from the kitchen.

A sudden loud beeping noise makes his hand jump slightly and spill his beer.

Tony carefully steps out into the garden holding a large ceramic platter. An enormous fish is on the platter, sitting on a base of crushed lentil Mejadra, a melange of sweetly spiced rice and lentils strewn with soft, fried onion, cumin and and fresh herbs. Balancing on the top is a variety of expertly sculpted vegetable flowers, a straggling of fresh pea shoots and some green things that Tony had foraged earlier from the Back Land. It is a culinary triumph. A true masterpiece deserving of a Michelin Star.

Gordon Ramsay would be proud.

'THE FISH IS SERVED!!!' says Tony grandly. Beads of sweat drip down his forehead.

Everyone stands up and claps, including the Zoom group although they can't see what the clapping is for. Tony smiles and bows.

'Tuck in everybody!!' says Tony. 'The fish won't wait!!'

He takes a long swig from a whisky bottle and staggers over to collapse in a green chair.

'Oooh lovely Tony, that's wonderful!' says Marge peering over the fish with delight.

'IS ANYBODY THERE? calls an urgent voice from over by the fence. 'WHAT'S GOING ON?'

Greg is feeling perturbed. He thought he heard a voice? There's nobody there. He stands up and starts to wander around the patio, but is distracted by a loud rustling in a nearby bush and some muffled shouting. Greg notices the bushes shaking and trembling. Then to his utter amazement the back end of a man appears, slowly crawling backwards out of the bush. He is shortly followed by another in a similar fashion. How many more men are there in this bush? They are not looking particularly happy and they are both covered in dead leaves. One of them is holding a large Nikon camera and the other is trailing a long quantity of string. Greg watches as they stand up and brush the twigs and leaves off themselves. They then get back down on their hands and knees again and peer back into the bush.

'I've got some lovely fishy treats…' one of them calls earnestly.

Greg is highly perplexed. Who are these men? What are they doing in the bush? Are they intruders? Should he do something?

'Oi!!! IS ANYBODY THERE?' Greg startles. There's that voice again. He is starting to think this is very odd indeed.

At the other side of the garden he spots a lady in dark glasses and a floppy hat appearing to be cutting the brambles. She is leaning forward over a laurel bush by the pond. Suddenly the lady loses her balance, tips forward and plunges head first into the bush. Greg hears a terrible high pitched scream. Good God!! He stands up in alarm. Then he notices a strange old man with a hunched back limping about over by the smaller lawn. Greg watches as he wanders over to the bush containing the lady, slowly bends down and after about 30 seconds he too disappears inside.

Greg is now feeling quite disturbed. Is there something in this beer that is clouding his judgement? He empties his glass onto the grass and refills it with a large stiff gin.

Greg can smell burning. Is that smoke coming out of the living room window? Is the house on fire? Should he do something? This is all very disturbing indeed. That voice is calling again... where is Jess? What's happened to the lady in the other bush and the limping old man? Greg is now on his second slice of brandy cake. His head is beginning to spin. He looks over at the living room windows and sees a dark monstrous figure standing there in the smoke like a demonic apparition.

'AAAAAAAAAAAHHHHHHHHH!!!!' he shrieks and spills his gin.

It is all too much. Greg's chest is constricting and he finds it hard to breathe. He flops heavily onto the lawn with a deep groan and lies flat on his face with his eyes firmly closed. The 'Vision of Hell' by Hieronymous Bosch pops into his head. In his mind's eye he is taking part in the grotesque scenes of torment as one of the more unfortunate characters. This is a living hell indeed.

Tony is pleased to notice Joe scooping up a large portion of salmon onto a plate. Good, he'll enjoy that! He takes it over to the lawn and puts it down on the grass.

Suddenly the cat comes running out of the bush. Tony's eyes widen in horror as he watches Chekhov tuck into his precious fish. Blast that wretched cat!!!

Tennessee Tim is ready. He has never looked so good. His new pale blue jump suit is a triumph. It is embellished with 1,567 red and white crystals, a long tassel feature at the shoulders, a fabulous faux gold belt and a cape detailed with a rising phoenix. A deep V cut at the front leaves a tantalising glimpse of Tim's delicately hairy chest into which the Mother-in-law has just rubbed a subtle fake tan in 'Moroccan sunset'.

It is a work of art. A creation that has taken the best of 23 episodes of Coronation Street, 123 cups of PG Tips, 284 Benson and Hedges and a bottle of Southern Comfort. The Mother-in-law feels a lump rise in her throat and a tear prick her eye as Tim launches himself out of the writing hut.

Elvis would be proud.

* * *

The Mother- in-law cranks the sound up to top volume, presses 'play' and the grandiose chords of 'Also Sprach Zarathustra' ring out into the evening air, heralding the coming of Elvis. A cluster of surprised wood pigeons leap up from the bushes and flutter away.

Everyone gathers around the stage on the lawn and waits with bated breath. Except for Tony who is reading his paper.

'How exciting!' says Marge.

Ten minutes later the tune rumbles on, but no Elvis is to be seen.

WEEK 7

It is not unusual for Tennessee Tim to keep his audience waiting, it is a tactic that he often uses to create a sense of suspense. But on this occasion Tim is having trouble with his left side burn. It has slipped slightly and has somewhat lost its sticky back pad. Luckily the Mother-in-law has packed an emergency Pritt Stick and he manages to solve the problem with a careful slick of the glue.

Finally he is ready. The moment has arrived. He leaps out from behind a tree trunk, wafts imperially around the lawn with his cape held aloft and glides seamlessly into a passionate rendition of 'Well that's Alright Mama'.

The audience gasp at this ethereal vision in pale blue, floating in the spot lights like an unusually large moth.

Tony glances up briefly from behind the Financial Times to inspect the proceedings. Good lord what on earth? What a nightmare! How did his daughter's musical taste sink so low? How could he have failed so miserably? All those concerts at Symphony Hall... what a waste! With a long sigh he settles back to a rather good article on Covid testing.

Jess has never seen anything more miraculous. Her eyes cloud over. It is 1972 and she is sitting at a round table in the banqueting suit of the Hilton Hotel in Vegas. It is a dinner-dine concert and she is sipping champagne under low lit chandeliers. There is a palpable electric charge in the air and the audience is on the edge of hysteria. Elvis in his pale blue jumpsuit is in ultimate form. Sleek, lithe, bursting with untamed energy and in complete control. But what's this? He is…jumping off the stage... coming towards her... kneeling at her feet…OH MY GOD… he is singing 'Can't Help Falling in Love'

…just for her. Of course, her rational brain knows it is not Elvis at all. It is Tennessee Tim from Smethwick. But that doesn't matter. Her amygdala thinks she has died and gone to heaven.

Tennessee Tim places a red nylon scarf around Jess's neck and moves back onto the lawn to sing a charismatic rendition of 'Polk Salad Annie'. Tim has spent many years honing his pelvic thrusting skills to a fine art and now is a perfect opportunity to show off his talents. It draws in the old ladies like moths to a flame.

Polk salad Annie, the gators got your granny

Everybody says it was a shame

Cause her momma was a workin' on the chain gang

A wretched, spiteful, straight-razor totin' woman

Lord have Mercy, pick a mess of it

Tim thrusts and grinds with mesmerising force. Tony is peering over the top of his paper. Marge has moved in for a closer look.

85 year old Mrs Parsons lives next door and can hear the noise drifting across her back garden. She comes out the back in her dressing gown. Whatever is going on? Is that Elvis? The sounds take her back to 1971 when she used to host those dinner dance parties. Those were the days. She remembers the white leather platforms she used to wear and Geoffrey's flared velvet suits. Eggnog. Yes! That's right! They used to drink eggnog! She would

spend hours making cheese and pineapple sticks. The things they used to do! She sighs sadly. Geoffrey has been in a care home for the past two years. He doesn't even recognise her anymore.

She puts one eye against a small hole in the fence. She can just catch a fleeting glimpse of pale blue.

'I CAN'T BLOODY SEE ANYTHING!!' screams an angry voice by the fence.

'That'll be your Aunty Sue, Jess can you turn her round,' says Marge.

Jess stands up, walks over to the computer and carefully turns it around.

'At long bloody last!' says Aunty Sue with a long sigh.

Chekhov is not pleased at all with this disruption to her peaceful evening. In a moment of madness she leaps out of the bush and up to the top branch of the Copper Beech tree. Oh dear! She finds herself stuck on a thick branch, looking down upon the horrified faces of Jeff and Joe. 'Miaoww,' she says.

'MIAAAEEEOOOOOOOWWWW!!'

Cap has managed to extract Avni from her landing spot inside the laurel bush. It was an unexpected fall and Avni is rather taken aback by the whole incident. Cap brings over a green chair and helps her to sit down. From their spot by the pond, Cap and Avni watch the proceedings on the large lawn.

2 hours later

Night is approaching and the sun begins her slow descent, bathing the pale sky in streaks of orange and gold. Riya has now gone back home with her daughters. Tim has had a half hour break during which he and the Mother-in law between them imbibe 6 bottles of Golden Ale, 4 glasses of Villa Vincini and 3 and a half slices of brandy cake. They are rather drunk.

Ada and Rowan have come down from the upstairs bedroom where they have been watching Netflix. They stand on the patio and observe the scene.

Marge is now on the stage in the arms of Tennessee Tim. They are singing 'Love me Tender'. She doesn't know the words, but it doesn't matter. It is quite awful. But rather marvellous.

Cap is slow dancing with Avni around the lawn. Greg is also on the lawn, propping up the Mother-in-law. She is very drunk and she slouches heavily on his shoulder. They are gently rocking to and fro.

'Ain't you a darlin',' she repeats over and over again into his ear.

Joe and Jeff are mentally and physically exhausted. They have finally given up trying to get the cat down from the tree and are now slowly revolving around the lawn together after consuming large quantities of damson gin. Chekhov is regarding them curiously from high up on the branch.

The Zoom family are clapping and singing along. Mrs Parsons is still peering through the hole in the fence.

Tony is in the kitchen rustling up some homemade mango and passionfruit ice cream. He has Beethoven's Fifth playing at top volume.

It is growing dark and the sun's last golden fingers are drifting away over the tree tops leaving a navy indigo sky. A large red moon peers through the branches of the Copper Beech.

PC Patel drives slowly down Chestnut Drive and notices rather a large number of vehicles parked in the drive. This looks suspicious. Very suspicious indeed. He parks up, gets out of his car and wanders up the driveway. He can hear the strains of music coming from the back garden. Is this a party? An illegal lockdown party? A party where he may find people breaking the two metre rule?

He knocks loudly on the front door. Nothing happens. He knocks again.

Someone in a large industrial mask opens the door. Smoke billows out from the hallway.

'Gonbhusiidhbhhhdhbc,' says the fire man through his mask.

'Hello I'm PC Patel. Are you the owner of this establishment?'

'Hjhdnnnkmkkggfffffffnnnnn,' replies the fire man.

PC Patel realises that this is going to get him nowhere. The billowing smoke is starting to make him cough. He decides to try round the back instead.

PC Patel opens the back gate and enters the garden. He is not prepared for the scene that awaits.

'Oh hello Officer!' says Marge. 'Would you like a dance?'

'What's going on here?' says PC Patel, his mouth falling open. 'This is a travesty!'

Tennessee Tim is belting out a drunken version of '*Lucy in the Sky with Diamonds*' at the request of Rowan (an avid Beatles fan) and there are several people flailing about on the lawn.

PC Patel looks about in disbelief. What on earth is going on? A large array of food... enormous quantities of alcoholic beverages... an Elvis impersonator ... singing The Beatles…people cavorting about… this is ALL WRONG!

'STOP!!!!!!' screams PC Patel at the top of his voice. Tim slowly and reluctantly grinds himself to a halt.

Tony pops out holding an ice cream cone.

'Oh hello Officer, would you like an ice cream?'

PC Patel has a face of thunder and a flash of lightening in his eyes. He storms over to Tim on the stage and snatches hold of the microphone. Everyone gathers around. Someone starts to clap.

'No, I would NOT like an ice cream,' he says, the microphone projecting his voice far and wide.

'It's very nice... mango and passionfruit,' says Tony.

'We are in a lockdown. LOCKDOWN!!! And I come over here to find what? Music? Singing? People dancing about all over the place! It's a disgrace! Look up there! See there! The moon! A big red moon! Do you know what that means? Do you?'

'It's night time?' suggests Marge helpfully.

'Ill met by moonlight indeed!' comments Tony giving his ice-cream a lick. It is rather delicious.

'Yes! Yes! Night time! That means you should all be in bed! Not cavorting about drinking and making merry! Look at you! And look at you! (pointing to Tim) A grown man in a pale blue baby grow! (There is a sound of shocked gasping). What do you think you're doing? Having a nice time are we? Enjoying ourselves are we? What about all the NHS workers eh? Are they having a nice time? Stuck on the Covid wards? Oh what a lovely time we're having!'

'I'm an NHS worker,' pipes up Marge.

'Well what about all the old people? All the old people stuck at home, going out of their minds with boredom? Are they having a nice time? No, no they're not!'

'Well I am,' calls Mrs Parsons from through the hole. 'I'm an old person and I'm having a lovely time!'

Everyone looks round. Who said that?

'Well... anyway. What about wearing masks? None of you are wearing masks!'

'Hnnjhhhjdbncmnnnnmmmmrrr,' says the fireman in his industrial mask, standing at the kitchen door looking like the Creature from the Black Lagoon.

'AAAAAAAAAHHHHHHHHHHHHHH,' shrieks Marge.

'Anyway this is a Lockdown and you should ALL be miserable. MISERABLE do you hear me? MISERABLE like everybody else in this bloody country. What would Boris say? Eh? What would he say if he could see you now?'

'Nothing at all! Look at Dominic Cummings!' says Tony sharply.

There is a sound of laughter and a few claps from the audience.

'You are all under arrest. Who is the proprietor of this sinister establishment?'

Everyone looks around in silence for a few moments. Then Cap the gardener speaks up.

'I am. I am the proprietor. This was all my idea. You can arrest me, Officer. No one else is to blame.'

'Cap!!' says Marge aghast.

'No,' says Avni finding an inner strength, 'it's me. It's all my fault. Arrest me!'

'Avni! No!!' says Marge.

'Hnnmcnjhbummmmnnn,' says the fire-man.

No-one could understand that.

Marge screams again at the sight of the fire-man, this time with such force that the cat, watching the proceedings from high up in the Copper Beech, panics and leaps dramatically though the air right onto the shoulders of PC Patel.

'Now THAT is one HELL of a cat!!!!' says Joe proudly.

In sheer terror, PC Patel collapses to the ground shielding his head.

'AAAAAAAHHHHHHHHHHHHH' he shrieks. 'This is an attack!!!!!'

'RUN EVERYBODY!!' shouts the Mother-in-law. 'RUN FOR YOUR LIVES!!!'

'RUN' shouts Aunty Sue from the computer. 'RUN!!!' shout all the other Zoom uncles and cousins. This is the one moment this evening when they realise the distinct advantage of being virtually rather than actually present.

'Wait for me!! I want to be arrested too!! I'm coming! This is the best thing that has happened to me since 1975!!' shouts Mrs Parsons from next door.

She touches up her lips with a spot of Chanel Rouge Allure Velvet Luminous Lip Colour in N°5, pops on her coat and shoes and rushes out of the house.

A scene of utter chaos ensues.

* * *

Jess and the two girls were the first to leave and headed straight down to the Esso station for much needed petrol.

WEEK 7

Tony managed to slip swiftly out of the house grabbing whatever he could on the way. He leapt with incredible deftness into his battered red Saab and sped off, tires screeching, into the night. Marge crept under the bush next to the pond and hid with Chekhov in a very clever spot. Cap and Avni were seen heading off down the garden and into the shadows.

The others weren't so lucky. It is 2am and Tennessee Tim, the Mother-in-law, Mrs Parsons, the fire-man, Joe, Jeff and Greg are now cooped up in a small cell at Thornhurst Road Police Station under the watchful eye of PC Patel. This will get him his promotion. For sure. Deputy Police chief Johnson will be proud.

Tennessee Tim starts to strum his guitar softly.

'Well isn't this wonderful!' says Mrs Parsons.

'Poor Edna,' says Joe, 'I bet she's missing us.'

'Don't worry Joe, I'm sure she'll be fine,' reassures Jeff.

'Hey Officer, come over 'ere...' calls the Mother-in-law.

'What's the matter?' says PC Patel.

'There ain't no trouble in having a little fun y' know. Wass your problem?' she says.

'We have to save the NHS,' says PC Patel. 'My Aunty Aisha, she's a nurse. She says it's bad.'

'I know iss bad. We ya'll knows iss bad. But there aint nothin' wrong with a bit o' happiness sometime. Besides, might be the lass day you ever 'ave.'

PC Patel ponders thoughtfully.

'Y' know maa son-in-low?' she points at Tennessee Tim. 'He raise faive hundre' an' feefty saix poun' tirty sayvern payance an' countin' for t' henhaychayss.'

'He did?' says PC Patel.

'Yeah and he make a whole lotta old folks 'appy. Why every Tursday the care 'ome dow' t' road open th' winders and let his music right in... they all singin' along like there's not a care in th' world!'

'Is that right?' says PC Patel. His heart is warming to this lady. He is starting to feel that he might have slightly overreacted.

'Yeah sure peoples are dyin', folks stuck in their 'omes goin' goddam crazy, but you juss gotta keep on fightin', keep on prayin'. It sure as hell ain't no good goin' round mopin'. That aint gonna help no-body.'

'What's your name?' says PC Patel.

'Why, my name's Phyllis, Officer.'

'Where are you from Phyllis?'

"Well aahm from Nashville Tennessee, Officer. Aah 'ere to take care o' maa precious boy. Ain't that right Son?' She blows a kiss at Tim.

'Well, it's very nice making your acquaintance Phyllis.'

'Same t' you, Officer.'

Tennessee Tim strums louder, '*The warden threw a party in the county jail...*'he sings.

'*The prison band was there and they began to wail...*'sings Joe suddenly livening up.

'*The band was jumpin' and the joint began to swing...*'joins in Jeff clicking his fingers.

'*You should've heard them knocked-out jailbirds sing,*' sings PC Patel. PC Patel!!!

And everyone in the small cell joins together in a chorus that would have brought the house down...

WEEK 7

Let's rock, everybody let's rock

Everybody in the whole cell block

Was dancin' to the Jailhouse Rock

* * *

Tony is sitting under a smallish bush to the left of the putting green at the 9th hole of Braisemere golf course. He is eating a slice of cake and swigging wine sporadically from a bottle of Zin. It's from Puglia, 2019. It is very fine.

Tony looks in his Tesco bag for something to read. Oh good God NO! He is horrified to discover that the magazine he thought was '*How to Spend it*' from this week's Financial Times, has turned out to be the May 2013 edition of the BMJ. He flicks through it and finds an article on 'spontaneous fungal peritonitis in patients with liver cirrhosis'. Oh well. That will have to do.

Bats dart and swoop playing chase with the fluttering moths. Tony listens to the birds' final evening calls before they settle down for the night. The dark silhouette of a lonely heron swoops low over the lake. The full moon gazes down at its own watery reflection. Just above Tony's left shoulder a lone spider carefully wraps a fly in a bag of fine silk.

The effects of the wine and the cake, sodden in brandy, are making Tony feel woozy and soporific. He creeps out of the bush and collapses flat on his back to look up at the wakening stars. A wandering woodlouse creeps over his outstretched left leg.

Spinoza could have been wrong. What if there is a God after all? Surely he will reveal himself tonight.

He imagines himself on Desert Island Discs, interviewed, of course, by the lovely Kirsty Young. This is his desert island moment. Alone for ever with no sign of human life for thousands of miles. *Hell is... other people.* Who was it who said that? Sartre? Pure and utter bliss. No-one to bother him. No appalling Elvis songs. Just the odd question from Kirsty here and there about his musical preferences. Of course in a perfect world he would have the complete works of Shakespeare and a recording of Rachmaninov's 2nd piano concerto. Instead he has a half drunk bottle of wine, some cake, a packet of nuts and an old BMJ. No matter. This is what freedom is all about.

* * *

Marge is in the kitchen trying to open a tin of beans. She has been struggling with the can opener for 15 minutes and has only managed to make a small hole. She pops on her slippers, opens the front door and heads next door to find Riya. Riya is a practical person, a person who is very capable of opening a tin of beans.

Success. Marge brings the opened can back, finds a spoon, pours a large Campari and settles down in front of the TV. Oh good, it's the Young Montalbano. Her favourite thing. Perfect.

Chekhov has consumed a very large fish that she found left on the table outside. She wanders in and settles down happily by Marge on the fluffy cushion on Tony's chair.

The next morning

Marge is in her dressing gown and bed socks listening to the 'Today Programme' on Radio Four. She is eating a large bowl of All Bran and yesterday's Daily Mail is open on her lap. There is a loud knock at the door. Marge puts down the paper and her bowl and shuffles to the door.

'Who is it?' she calls.
'It's me.'
'Are you the police?'
'No! It's me. Let me in!'
'Is that you Tony?'
'Of course it bloody well is. Let me in!'
Marge opens the door.
'Hello Tony!' says Marge.
Tony gives Marge a peck on the lips.
'Have you seen my glasses? I've lost them,' says Tony.
'I think I saw them on the sofa... let me have a look...'

* * *

It is lunch time and Tony has gone to the Back Land to forage for some green things to add to his soup. He is surprised to notice the head of Cap the gardener appear at the window of the writing hut. The window opens and Cap's head pops out.

'Good afternoon, Dr. Pinkton would you mind letting me out. The door has got stuck.'

'Hello, Cap. Yes of course!' says Tony taking hold of the handle and pulling hard.

The door swings open. Cap steps out of the hut. He is

shortly followed by Avni.

Tony raises his left eyebrow slightly. Cap has rather gone up in his estimation.

'Thank you so much for a lovely evening,' she says to Cap.

'Remember dear lady,' he says, 'if your lawn needs cutting, just call and I will be there immediately.'

Cap takes her hand and bows gallantly.

'Oh it will! And most likely quite soon!' replies Avni. There is a lightness about her and certain sparkle in her eyes that Tony hadn't noticed before.

Cap and Avni walk off down the garden leaving Tony to gather his greens.

Week 8

Tony and Marge are sitting on the green garden chairs on the patio, sipping wine. It is evening and the birds are chirping their final goodnight calls. A new moon, a silver bow, hangs high above the Copper Beech. A lone owl screeches. The sky is turning indigo blue and pale moths are flapping about the kitchen window. 'Tis almost fairy time.

'There's so much time, Tone.' says Marge wistfully. 'This Lockdown is going on for ever.'

'No Marge, there's so little time.' says Tony. 'Nothing goes on for ever.'

'Well it seems endless to me,' says Marge. 'What are we to do with all this time?'

'There's always something to do. Always jobs to be done.'

'Yes, you're right. There's always something.'

'The only time we really have is now Marge. Right now. In this very moment.'

'This very moment,' repeats Marge.

'Just be, Marge. Just…be.'

Just then, faint sounds of singing voices drift over the tree tops. It gathers, swells and grows louder.

'Listen!' says Marge. 'Can you hear it?'

'I can hear something...' says Tony straining his ears to listen.

'This all feels just like a dream. Nothing but a dream.'

She starts to sway and hum softly.' My mother loved this song...'

'Dance with me Marge!' says Tony standing up suddenly. After all, as Spinoza would say, *reason is no match for passion.*

'Oh Tone!' says Marge.

Tony and Marge dance and turn slowly round the darkening lawn, wine glasses in hand, to the soft sounds of distant singing...

We'll meet again, don't know where, don't know when

But I know we'll meet again some sunny day.

Unheard upstairs is the sound of the grandfather clock. 'Tick... tick... tick,' it goes, like the comforting sound of a heartbeat. And look at that! It's five minutes past 1 o' clock!

Epilogue

Tennessee Tim posted the photos on Facebook from the party that Jeff took with his Nikon camera, and his fan base has now increased dramatically. He has entered the 2021 Elvis Championships at the NEC and is a firm favourite to win. He has a whole new wardrobe including a jumpsuit in royal purple and belt with his name engraved in genuine 22 carot gold. He is taking the Mother-in-law for a surprise trip to Graceland next year for her birthday. So far he has raised a total of £3567.67 for the NHS. Priscilla now has her own instagram page and has over 10,000 followers. She still eats Sheba.

Joe and Jeff have developed a whole new angle on 'Rainbow Paws'. Their Zoom quizzes were such a hit that they are now running them every week and raising money to open their own home for abandoned cats. Their face mask designs were spotted by the assistant lead designer at Versace and they are now being developed for launch at the 2021 Paris catwalk collection. Edna now has her own fashion label and is modelling her own designs. She will be appearing as a special guest on 'This Morning' next month. She is currently on a diet.

Cap and Avni have formed a successful local gardening company offering services to the locals. Cap manages the lawns while Avni develops the borders and flower beds. They also offer holistic nature-healing therapy workshops with weekend residencies in the Wyre Forest. They make an excellent team.

Sergeant Patel. Yes he did indeed get his promotion. He is now a well respected Sergeant in the local community known for supporting charity events and fundraisers. He is a particularly popular character at the Children's Hospital where he entertains the children by dressing up in various costumes and doing tricks. He has a wonderfully talented costume designer known as Phyllis from Nashville Tennessee. His Aunty Aisha is very proud of him.

Mrs Parsons has a whole new lease of life visiting prisoners at the local prison. She listens to their stories and receives and replies to their letters. At Winston Grey Prison she is known fondly as 'Jail Bird Sally'. She is publishing a collection of stories called 'Tales from the Jail' which will be out soon. She likes to wear white platforms and has a particular fondness for eggnog.

Riya is now very busy everyday making lunches for the officers down at Thornhurst Road police station. Her samosas have won the 'Best in Brum' award for excellence and her success was highlighted on Midland's Today. She was particularly delighted to meet Nicholas Owen.

After several months of Gestalt therapy, Greg is well on the road to recovery from the events of the birthday party and has taken up painting. He particularly enjoys creating intricate apocalyptic scenes from the Book of Revelation. He is planning an exhibition next summer.

Jess continues her work teaching adults at the college.

EPILOGUE

She is now allowed to go in to work and had a happy reunion with all her learners. Her Lockdown story was published and is particularly popular amongst cat lovers. King's Heath Cat Club have now ordered more than 150 copies. She continues to see Marv at the Esso station and they are working together on a book called, '*Crystals and the Art of Positive Thinking.*' It will be available soon on Amazon.

Rowan has returned to University in London and is enjoying her evenings in the pub with her friends. She has started a micro brewery in her student lodgings. Ada has returned to school and is enjoying being with her friends again, although sadly it is much harder now to cheat in exams.

Tony has finished his book, '*My life with Spinoza*' at long last. It has been published by Penguin and has had an excellent review in the Times Literary Supplement. It is on Richard and Judy's list of top ten books to read this season.

Marge continues her work with her patients. She was finally given a computer by the hospital which works like a dream. In fact after making copious notes at training sessions she is now an expert on Zoom and MST. She has joined the IT team as an advisory consultant. She still collects sticks.

Chekhov continues to live with optimism and curiosity. She spends her days watching the wildlife from her hiding spot in the bush, her evenings hoping for fish and her nights sleeping on Tony's chest.

The End

Kate Egawa is a teacher and artist. She is currently studying for an MSc in Psychotherapy. She lives in Birmingham with her two daughters and Kewpie the cat.

Printed in Great Britain
by Amazon